T0195072

MAN

ON A

CAMEL

DUNCAN CULLMAN

authorHOUSE®

AuthorHouse™
1663 Liberty Drive
Bloomington, IN 47403
www.authorhouse.com
Phone: 833-262-8899

Published by AuthorHouse   03/03/2021

ISBN: 978-1-6655-1884-0 (sc)
ISBN: 978-1-6655-1883-3 (hc)
ISBN: 978-1-6655-1882-6 (e)

Library of Congress Control Number: 2021904585

CONTENTS

MAN ON A CAMEL 15

Given the likelihood of Hannibal rising

Against "corporate interests" in a protracted war

To eradicate corruption and corporate irresponsibility

For the sake of human survival and the people who will absorb the higher new cost of living,

While espousers of the Green New Deal pledge allegiance to the principal,

Who will be left standing to boycott Walmart and its discounted prescriptions?

This brings us back full circle to the reality

Of industrial automation—that man is lazy

While self-destructive in nature, the beast being within us,

So that the very rich mock us for dreaming of some different economic plan than wealth.

We saints who dream of a better world are dreaming of a distant heaven while waiting for our departure.

We no longer fit in here in this power grab of Wall Street.

Be a worker: stand guard at your factory.

Be a nurse: the planet is dying—console it in your arms; inject drugs.

Be a poet: write verses for Beethoven Junior.

Be a doctor: prescribe happy pills so everyone will die happy.

In this sunset of the human race, is there even any hope left,

Or will this all become one vast Sahara?

Your camel is patiently waiting for a signal that you intend to cross,

To find an oasis of happiness where you will watch *Ozzie and Harriet*.

Meet your neighbors; they are all singing like Ricky Nelson,

"My China doll down in old Hong Kong."

She is no longer waiting there for you; she has left with the Imperial Fleet

Down in East Africa, where the flamingos have taken off.

The waitress you married ran away with the dishwasher to live in a trailer park

Very happily with your former children, who now think you are a sex offender.

Why bring anyone at all into this decaying world?

Here we suffer to earn grace, and the very wise would trade all their wisdom just to be young again.

Start a newspaper, be an editor, write an obituary column—

They were great people, but they died.

Life here is an almost impossible situation from day one,

Unless your father is some corporate president,

Whereas with proper education, you might rise up to be vice president

Of this grand corporation, which pays no tax and is

Exempt from responsibility to people.

LOVE IS THE ONE GLUE: NO OTHER GLUE BONDS

On the passing of my friend

There is only one glue that bonds all creation.

My loving friend has passed away just yesterday;

Now he is like a horse gone to the glue factory,

The summation of his great love for us all

Displayed most valiantly by his leadership

That he passed on to us, his unique understanding

Of all this creation. Our daily life we have just today;

Live it as though it might be your last.

One day, you will be right, and it will indeed be your last.

Then the victory of your love shall return to your Creator God;

It all came from him through your fathers and mothers.

Abraham could not live well without God, who is love;

Neither can you for very long, nor I.

We will all be old horses done at the racetrack,

All shipped off to the glue factory to help bond the universes.

Love is the one glue, and it only comes by faith:

"Believe in me, your One God; I am the author of everything good.

"Without my love, you will self-destruct like Hamlet, like Caesar."

I have written this to all who have died and gone on before us,

In loving memory of their sacrifice on the Cross.

They all crossed our lives by love, and we intersected

On the critical highway whereby we found each other to be friends.

We were sometimes critical friends, and we were misunderstood—

Mostly by those who daily misunderstand God, who sent us.

God has given all of us to you to guide you by friendship,

So when someone speaks to you, please take note:

It is our One God who gives us this day for our awakening.

Wash your face clean, because you need to see and hear and feel

The love that is coming your way this very minute.

Our One God is powerful and has sent you one more friend.

In Walmart, you look for things to buy, but these cannot buy happiness.

You have gone shopping today because you need a friend to help steer you

Into the new better direction in your life (Bill McCollom steered us to compassion for each other), away from doubt and fear.

We must not be afraid, and neither was Jesus entering Jerusalem.

There are those who think differently from us; the world is ignorant still,

Yet we will reach heaven in the end because we find friends.

They are not just people who praise us; they are much more—people who offer advice.

Love is the one glue—no other bonds—and love is critical.

Therefore, the holy prophets were critical of the many ignorant people.

They offered friendly advice, but of course the heathen took no notes.

When someone asks for money, give him or her advice as well, like a friend.

This love we share is our true measure and what we were born for.

Believe that God loves you, and be saved.

MI AMIGO ES UN PERRO LLAMADO RUSIO

Mi amigo es un perro llamado Rusio

Vive en un país llamado Chile

Que está en forma más o menos como un espagueti

En el norte es muy seco y es un desierto

En el sur de Chile, donde llueve mucho Rusio vive en Villarrica.

A veces, en invierno nieva en Chile, pero por lo general en las altas montañas de los Andes

Pero a veces nieva en baja en las ciudades.

Nadie sabe de dónde vino de Rusio, solamente Rusio

Hace apenas un año hoy que llegó al pueblo .probable fue abandonado por una mala irresponsable propietario

Fue descubierto por primera vez por temprano turística del amanecer que se percató de que el perro tiene hambre y se dirigió al mercado cercano a él comprar un poco de comida para perros y aperitivos

El torist fue a dormir muy triste esa noche porque estaba preocupado por su nuevo amigo el perro llamado Rusio.

Rusio fue nombrado un recogido para el perro por varios comerciantes locales porque era un perro de pelo corto rubio por lo que le dio un nombre que significa rusa.

Rusio había parece tener un amigo que es otro perro llamado Oranginho que se colorea como una naranja (y probablemente un perro chino Chow) .Oranginho sigue Rusio todas partes corren de lado a side. Oranginho quiere saber dónde Rusio está recibiendo su comida.

Alguien ha estado alimentando Rusio carne y la carne asada beef.Is de TI a la señora Madelyn en Artes Sur que vende sombreros de lana y calcetines? ¿O es la dama Michelle que vende cuencos de madera? Ella vino aquí desde Francia por amor y se casó, pero su marido falleció .o es que Giovanni del cocinero en Balganez Restaurante donde el negocio es lento en la temporada de invierno, o es el mismo turista que come tortas kuchen en Kuchenladen con su té de la tarde?

Debido a que una nube de gas de olor dulce sigue Rusio donde quiera que se goes.That qué Oranginho lo sigue everywhere.He quiere ser tan popular como Rusio que al parecer tiene amigos en todas partes por toda la ciudad, pero gruñe ahora en Oranginho a favor de pie fuera de su camino y no asfixiarlo.

¿Quién, por ejemplo, ha comprado Rusio el nuevo collar de cuero verde de guisantes con colgando Milk bones miniatura? Todo el mundo ama Rusio a pesar de que no tiene casa, pero sólo se pasea por toda la ciudad.

Vamos a ver si podemos encontrar Rusio una buena casa en algún lugar en el que pueda estar caliente y no morir de hambre, donde los coches no se le atropellado en la calle!

Él es mi amigo Rusio y él es un perro! Traerlo a casa a alguien por favor! Y me traen a casa también, soy una persona sin hogar llamado Agostino.We toda la necesidad de ser amado y encontrar un hogar para protegernos de las tormentas

MY FRIEND IS A DOG NAMED RUSIO

My friend is a dog named Rusio.

He lives in a country called Chile,

Which is shaped roughly like a strand of spaghetti.

In the north, it is very dry and is a desert.

In the south of Chile, where Rusio lives in Villarica, it rains a lot.

Sometimes in winter, it snows in Chile—usually only in the high Andes Mountains

But sometimes down low in the towns.

No one knows where Rusio came from, only Rusio.

Just a year ago today he arrived in town; probably he was abandoned by an irresponsible, bad owner.

He was discovered first by one nearly dawn tourist, who noticed the hungry dog and went to the nearby market to buy him some dog food and snacks.

The tourist went to sleep very sad that night because he was worried about his new friend, the dog named Rusio.

Rusio is a named picked for the dog by various local shopkeepers. He is a blond, short-haired dog, so they gave him a name that means Russian.

Rusio seems to have a friend, another dog named Oranginho, who is colored like an orange (and probably a Chinese Chow). Oranginho follows Rusio everywhere; they run side by side. Oranginho wants to know where Rusio is getting his food.

Someone has been feeding Rusio steak and roast beef. Is it the lady Madelyn in Artes Sur who sells wool hats and socks? Or is it the lady Michelle who sells wooden bowls? She came here from France for love and married, but her husband passed away. Or is it Giovanni, the cook at Balganez Restaurant, where business is slow in the winter season? Or is it that same tourist, who eats kuchen tortas at Kuchenladen with his afternoon tea?

You see, a cloud of sweet-smelling gas follows Rusio wherever he goes. That is why Oranginho follows him everywhere. He wants to be popular like Rusio, who seemingly has friends everywhere all over the town but growls now at Oranginho to please stand out of his way and not smother him.

Who, for instance, has bought Rusio the new pea-green leather collar with dangling miniature milk bones? Everyone loves Rusio even though he has no home but just wanders around the entire town.

Let's see if we can find Rusio a nice home somewhere where he can be warm and not starving, where no cars will run him over in the street!

He is my friend Rusio, and he is a dog. Bring him home, someone, please!

And bring me home too. I am a homeless person named Agostino. We all need to be loved and find a home to shield us from the storms!

WHAT ARE BEARS?

Bears Visit Santiago, a Children's Book

"What are bears doing in Santiago?"

Bears eat berries.

Bears love honey.

When it's cold, bears hibernate.

Then they wake up hungry!

"What's all that noise?" ask the curious bears.

"There's a city down there in all that smog and noise!"

"There are many garbage cans surrounded by barking dogs!"

The dogs stop barking when the sun rises to warm the sidewalk.

"Now that the dogs are asleep we can go to Santiago," say the bears.

"We don't have wallets, so nobody can rob us on the subway."

"We don't have backpacks, so nobody can pick through them while we walk."

"We don't have passports, so they won't think we're rich gringo tourists."

"What do we need taxis for?" proclaim the bears.

"We are bears! We go where we want to go!"

The policeman lets them cross the street.

The cars stop, and people stare at them.

The signs all say, "Don't feed the bears!"

The grocery man throws oranges at them and runs away.

"We want the blueberries, and look, some peanuts!"

"Bears eat anything at all and everything," say the passing schoolchildren.

"Run," says their teacher. "Run, children, run!"

"We're not scared of bears," say the children.

(Fear is something they accidentally taught us in school.)

"We're not afraid either!" say the hungry bears.

"Look, the supermarket shelves are empty."

Bears don't even carry credit cards.

Dogs have woken up now from all this commotion;

Dogs are barking wildly in the street.

"Let's go home," say the bears.

"Follow that bus that says San Jose de Maipo," says Papa Bear.

"Yes, that's the bus," says Mama Bear.

The bus driver sees the bears, stops the bus, and runs to the subway.

"Board the bus, all my cubbies!" says Papa Bear.

"Mama Bear didn't lose her license. She can drive!"

All the bears go home to Cajon de Maipo, where they climb,

And climb some more, up and up,

Into the mighty Andes Mountains.

"There are no bears in Chile!" says a policeman. (He doesn't understand climate change.)

"We know better. We are the bears!"

MORNING HAS COME AND WILL WE MOVE FORWARD?

Another fresh morning,

This one with red clouds; sailor, take warning.

I suppose all the stories I made from my past are really like

Confederate statues. I had mostly lost that war of my selfish desires.

Now am I to tear them all down and forget my life and forget who I am?

My history has made me; this is who I am, where I came from.

No history, no memory, no guidance for the future,

The United States, an unguided missile

Careening wildly into a new, troublesome future with Alzheimer's.

Its police became a society unto themselves, separate and detached from reality,

Imagining all nonpolice to be criminals sneaking about organizing revolutions.

"Sunday Worship Service, Police Only."

"There are those who will not join us and are demons."

"They practice heresy disguised as politics while looting and protesting."

"They will not declare their outside income, mostly from drug smuggling and sex trafficking."

"Their sons and daughters go to the finest schools to learn how to be gangsters like their president."

Now is the time for all police to rise up and stranglehold them to the pavement!

Now is the time for excessive paranoia because *everyone* is a *terrorist*!

"What about integration?" Who said that?

Integrate politicians with people and police with citizens. Or is it too late for that?

Have we lost the way?

"There will be war on the Italian Peninsula. The poor will revolt and follow Hannibal, the rich who oppress them, Caesar Octoberus."

ACADIA RISING

The United States is falling down,

Whereas Acadia is rising up

To cover over the mantel of corruption.

Too many senators, their pockets stuffing;

Too many corporations placing profits ahead of our enviro.

Something's gotta give in this cataclysm of self-destruction.

Is man suicidal with his existential greed?

His tragic flaw in this soap opera that will end with his demise?

Then let him fall.

Lobsters and porpoises serve more compatible purposes.

Acadia is rising. There will be a new dawn;

There will be a new earth.

The heavens will prevail and send man into exile

For his transgressions, such as burning fossil fuel unrepentantly.

He will be banished from this earth

To fly away to a very distant planet.

Will he have learned his lesson? I think not,

Because his pact is with Lucifer,

His hometown is Salem.

Now the whole earth will burn.

Even so, Acadia will rise up magnificent.

Prophecy fails, whereas love does not—never.

That is why we are here to love.

Love also this earth, for there is no other like it.

Love and live.

THE HUNT FOR
MENGELE

JOSEF MENGELE WAS BORN INTO A FAMILY THAT MANUFACTURED TRAILERS that were pulled behind trucks and cars and horses. The family had been in the business probably since the days of Otto von Bismarck, who united Germany in 1871.

He was an avid alpinist, skier and ice climber. Josef Mengele was born around 1905 in Westphalia by the Rhine River near the French and Luxembourg border. Josef enlisted in the ski troops mountain division, as he was thirty-four years old when Germany invaded Poland. The draft was compulsory in the New Nazi Germany of Adolf Hitler, who proclaimed himself "führer" or leader. That was that, as democracy was blamed for most of the world's ills and was now replaced of necessity by the German people, an Aryan race, destined to rule the planet. This happened soon after the 1936 Olympics in Berlin, where Germany won the most medals, sweeping everything but the track event won by an American negro, Jesse Owens.

Mengele's division was quickly attached to the German Fifth Panzer Division, assigned to break out the entrapped Wehrmacht Army of General Joachim Von Paulus. His army was surrounded by the Russian Army at Stalingrad, led in the end by General Nikita Kruschev, who would one day be the premier of the USSR, as well as Communist Party boss.

It was a very cold winter, that one in Russia 1941/1942, and the tanks of the 5th Panzer Division attacked northward in snow and ice but ran out of the precious ingredients for their engine's ethanol, which the Germans were first to produce. Their petroleum supplies were running very low after General Rommel's defeat in Africa. The 5th Panzer Division came to a grinding halt then and there, unable to move when the Red Army discovered its position and lobbed every imaginable projectile destroying most of the division's heavy tanks.

Josef Mengele jumped onto the turret of one burning Panzer and pulled more than two *komeradden* to safety. He became a war hero and was transported back to field hospitals and then to his hometown to recuperate from his burns.

His wife later declared that Josef's ambition had overcome his reason when his old professor telegraphed him to ask for his assistance at Auschwitz Internment and reeducation facility in Poland. He acquiesced and departed thereafter in 1944 to play a leading role in "The Final Solution," which Hitler and Heinrich Himmler, a chicken farmer, had drafted for the extermination of every Jew in Europe.

Often Hitler's motorcade stopped by a small, picturesque lake near Rosenheim. There, the führer would enjoy a picnic on his rides between Munich and his residence at the Eagle's Nest, which had a view of often snowy mountains. The führer detested the winter and its snow, preferring summers with the frivolous Eva Braun and their dogs, Blondie the German shepherd being one.

Mengele became quite engrossed injecting gasoline into twins of the Jewish race that he had saved for his experiments. Sometimes he injected substances into their eyeballs to change their colors. He even had a collection of these various eyeballs of different colors on his office wall, after they were removed and soaked in formaldehyde most likely. He also saved an eight-year-old white Russian-looking Jewish girl, possibly named Nona Okun. He sterilized her and kept her in his office as a pet or companion for his loneliness, as his wife remained at home in Westphalia, sending him letters bearing the family news:

Dear Josef,

You must remember the kindly neighbors whose sons were sent to the Russian front in Operation Barbarossa to give us all "Breathing Room" [as Hitler called it]. Well, the news is bad as they haven't returned. But they did at least die for the glory of the Fatherland [Germany] to defeat those barbaric Bolsheviks.

The girlfriend of Mengele was shipped to another camp perhaps one that was quickly liberated by Russian troops, so she quite possibly survived.

This brings me to Nona Okun, who was tall and skinny and looked like a white Russian but was from a kibbutz in Israel. She arrived in Portillo, Chile, proclaiming herself to be an alpine ski racer from New York State (which she had visited briefly).

At any rate, maybe as a child in Russia, she had cross-country skied in gymnasium class or the like in the USSR before escaping to Israel.

I was sixteen years old when I met her and she confided to me, "I was in Argentina in a small town. And suddenly, there in the same town, Mengele came walking across the sidewalk after buying a newspaper. I was astonished to see him still alive and in better health than me. I wondered, How had he escaped capture?"

As a ten-year-old child I had read William Shirer's *Rise and Fall of the Third Reich*, all 1,100 pages describing atrocities committed by Nazi doctors in the name of medicine—freezing couples in bathtubs and on and on.

Nona wanted me to be friendly to the tall blond German man on one ski with his one leg and arm stabilizers with little skis attached. She told me to go up the ski lift with him, as he would, without doubt, invite me to visit Bariloche, Argentina. Bariloche had now become a Nazi hideout. And Dr. Mengele was sure to show up there, as he was attached to this one-legged German, Hans Ullrich Rudel (a Stuka pilot).

Rudel explained on the ski lift that, if I wanted to visit, I should please ask the Chilean ski team chaperone, Mrs. Leatherby-Gazitua if I could travel across the frontier from Chile to Argentina. I was a minor, which meant that, without an adult accompanying me, I would be unable to cross borders.

Just three months prior in Alpine Meadows, California, I had ridden up the ski lift there with this very same man. But maybe, I thought, this was his twin brother or something four thousand miles south. Or did he fly everywhere like a bird?

★★★

My own father would one day ask me why I had decided to conspire with these foreign terrorists. "Just exactly what was in it for you?" he drilled me at the dinner table out of the clear blue sky ten years later when I went to visit him in Connecticut, years after his involvement with the CIA.

The plan that was formulated by Rudel and Mrs. Leatherby was that I was to take the narrow-gauge train, the only train in Chile, from the South Metropolitan Station to Osorno, where I was to meet up with my Chileans ski team friends. Among them were Veronica Saez, who would one day marry a Chilean Army general, and Ricardo "Dickie" Leatherby and his chaperone mother, who would later save my life.

After sharing my banana with Mapuche children in the South Station, I boarded the train. And to my surprise, the one-legged man came walking by, finding me. I felt uncomfortable, but then he invited me to the front of the train, where I shoveled some coal into the engine. It was a steam locomotive. Then the conductors and Rudel told me to go back to my seat.

In Osorno, I departed and told the taxi driver the name of the hotel Mrs. Leatherby was to pick me up from the next morning. The Chilean ski team had gone ahead of us, but Mrs. Leatherby had decided to spend a night or two at the various hotels at each end of the Lake of All the Saints, Lago de Todos los Santos, east of the Volcano Osorno but west of Cerro Tronador, also a volcano but thought to be dormant now. In those olden days in the Andes, there were no plowed roads, and crossing the Southern Andes was only possible by a sled caboose pulled on a chain by a bulldozer between several lakes, below the snowline usually.

There was now no sign of the one-legged pilot. He had rushed forward with the Chilean ski team to arrive in Bariloche quickly, as he was a ski race official, president of the German Ski Club. The Chileans were told his club was off limits. It was well known the tables in the living room there featured mostly booklets printed by the German

SS, featuring pictures of killings of the non-German enemies—Poles, Russians, Bulgarians, and Serbs.

Mengele was arriving in Bariloche according to my Israeli friends at Portillo, who were also on their way to capture Mengele by camping out in the rainy-snowy Patagonia winter. This would be very challenging for them, as Israel is a desert country, where Jesus and His disciples were rarely engulfed in Seattle-like rain and snow. In my first week in Argentina, it decided to snow four feet and then rain for a week and melt it all. Then it changed back to snow and then to rain.

The houses in Bariloche and Villa Angostura and San Martin de Los Andes all had excellent roofs and well-stocked metal stoves. In those early years, one added coal at night, just like in New Hampshire sixty years ago.

Mengele had heard about extradition papers for war crimes signed by West Germany for his arrest and sold his carpenter shop in Olivos, a suburb of Buenos Aires, two weeks before the Israeli team that kidnapped Eichmann arrived to abduct him as a second target. Mengele eluded them all and fled to Asuncion, Paraguay, where he lived in a nice German chalet.

West Germany learned of his whereabouts and signed extradition papers sent to Paraguay, so Mengele soon traveled to Brazil. En route, he managed to steal some identification papers off some resident with a German last name, whose picture looked amazingly similar to his own. His family in Germany kept sending him dividends from the family trust fund, so he never quite ran out of money but was close to that when he met a friendly German Brazilian couple near Sao Paulo but in the highlands. The man went off to the city to work every week. Mengele stayed home and screwed his wife. This was where Mengele went between trips to Bariloche yearly to go ice climbing in Bariloche.

The Mengele I saw in Bariloche was definitely this cornered animal of a man, fighting, on the run, hunted by thirty governments and the relatives of six million dead Jews. Of course there were those who didn't really care about finding such a monster and were hoping just the opposite.

I was riding up the lift with an Argentine who pointed at the skier below us doing stem christies and told me, "That one is Mengele!"

I was a young ambitious ski racer, and although I found all this about Mengele intriguing, I was by now hoping not to meet him as well.

Mengele had escaped capture in Germany because his two grandparents, born in New York, were possibly not even German. So the SS had not given him the tattoo of racial purity, which the Allies were looking for on all the arms of every captured German at the end of World War II.

General Dwight David Eisenhower, the US general of all combined Allied Operations, ordered every former German SS officer to be interred in the very same concentration camps where they had exterminated the Jews and Untermenschen. Then Dwight David Eisenhower failed to send these German prisoners any food, so they starved to death in three weeks.

Mengele, of course, was never captured. The body of this man whose identification papers he used was dug up in Brazil near where he had died of a heart attack. This was after he'd been rescued from drowning in an undertow while swimming by his German friend (whose wife he screwed). It turned out to be Mangele. He had eluded everyone but the ocean itself and died there in 1971.

THE VERY LAST
AMATEURS

I WOULD LIKE TO DESCRIBE US AS THE VERY LAST OF THE AMATEURS. WE WERE encamped on the side of Mount Washington just below lower "Lower Snowfields" on the flats there where sometimes the river backs up and floods if it rains for more than a day. Skippy, my companion and friend, had found the army tent somewhere or borrowed it. It had no floor, but there were spruce bows for that. Most of that very well-tented area had been denuded of the lower branches of all spruce trees. Nowadays that's not the case, as the US Forest Service has banned camping up there since 1969. But it was 1968 when I had made my triumphal return to Mount Washington, which taught me how to ski "modern."

Due to the grace and benevolence of my father (who had adopted me), I had received ski lessons and ski coaching from "Miki" Clemens Hutter from Salzburg, Austria. He taught me to ski "the Austrian way"— wedeln as it was defined by Kruckenhauser, who preached skis in parallel as the only correct technique. Mount Washington, albeit Tuckerman's Ravine and Hillman's Highway, were teaching me differently.

From our tent location below Dodge's Drop, we could see ski tracks up there carved by Brooks Dodge, who had finished fourth place in the 1956 Olympic slalom. If I would have known that at the time, I would have followed him everywhere, even though our introduction to one another one time had not gone well.

Nobody paid Brooks Dodge to ski those death-defying chutes, and nobody was paying me either. I was not yet twenty-one and not of legal age at twenty to inherit anything.

Skipper spent most of each day listening to various skiers' big adventure stories and smiling enthusiastically but adding his last line as they packed their belongings to head down the mountainside for home. "You don't have to carry all that heavy food home with you unless of course you must!"

Very well spoken by Skipper (Franklin Corning Stevens, Jr.) at least five times daily. Four out of five departing mountaineers would leave us their food but not their beer very often. So for beer, which was one commodity necessary for Skipper, we went to town once a week or whenever it ran out.

There was also an Arab down there in North Conway named "Woody," who it was rumored worked for "the Man." We did odd jobs upon occasion for Woody to earn beer money, such as clearing building lots and burning brush. But it was usually a Korean War vet named Chet who ran the chainsaw. Chet thought I looked like a gook, as I had the high-set eyebrows and or high cheekbones of an American Indian or something. I stayed away from Chet, as the war had made him nuts.

"That wasn't a war, Chet! That was the Korean Conflict." You wouldn't want to say that too loudly to Chet's face.

So then me and Skipper Skippy Stevens took turns lugging the two cases of beer back up the mountainside. Sometimes Skippy sold a single can for $5, which was the going price at 5,000 feet elevation. We only once climbed to the 6,288-foot summit, as the weather up there turned deadly with high wind and below freezing temperatures even in late May.

Of course the snow mostly melted by June, and so we left for the lowlands of the Conways where the girls our age were putting on tennis shorts and bathing suits to dip in Lake Conway.

Thus, in the spring of 1968, I only lived at Tuckerman Ravine ten weeks and skied on average two to four runs per day about five days per week. We sat a lot in the lunch rocks and drank beer, Skippy five to my one probably. I made over eighty or ninety ski runs on Mount Washington that one spring. It was the year before the 1969 Mount

Washington Inferno Ski Race, held for the first time since 1939, as the weather on the summit of that mountain was never very cooperative.

There were some young girls who would spend the night with me there in my sleeping bag, though the very next morning, they usually departed without skiing to find a hot bath at home in the valley below. Our accommodations were primitive at best, and because people urinated in the dark of night without venturing very far into the woods, we often had to move the tent to a fresher-smelling location.

Of course the US Forest Service put an end to us mountainside residents, as the environment was being ecologically upset. The Hell's Angel Motorcycle Club. Or some chapter of it anyway, began camping out up there maybe fifty yards away through the woods, dropping LSD and other drugs as well. We knew Richard Nixon and the various powers, like Harvard University and Ski Club had a dismal view of most motorcycle afficionados without college degrees.

GOD WHO IS LOVE

Great Glory and Honor to God, Who is Love.

Great glory and honor to the Creator of Love, Whose love we are afforded to share

Among our families and friends and also the strangers we meet.

When they beg for money, we comply with quarters, dimes, and nickels or food;

We are honored that we fall among those so honored by God to have received love.

Kindly we pass on God's free gift to the law-abiding and chosen.

In even hostile lands, where there is danger and lawlessness,

We bring tidings of joy and peace, we establish hope and salvation—

All this sent from our God, through us His radiant love dispersed.

Here in this otherwise dark world we shine forth like the sun breaking forth from behind dark clouds.

ST. LITTLETON

For the kingdom of heaven is like an unhappy man living in a tiny town.

It's more imperative that we focus on and appreciate what we have

round him and criticize everyone and everything he sees.

So he exclaims, "What a wretched little town this is, so very small, and everyone here is a loser!"

It is his own shortsightedness that makes him belittle his tiny town.

It would be better for him to rename his tiny town "St. Littleton,"

Because every street corner is full of potential saints.

Such a rotten world we live in if we think it so.

Yet, in the eyes of God, it is His perfection and His plan

That we rise up and overcome to be the heroes He wants us to be.

We are all potentially His saints in the making through His Grace.

We are reformed only by trial and tribulation.

Thus, we each fight a personal Armageddon daily!

My brother and sister saints, now I behold your struggles;

If I were only better able to discern and see your saintliness in the making,

Then I might become a happier man and be more gleeful and saintly.

"Oh, my dear saintly brothers and sisters, how I empathize with your mundane daily struggles."

In the final day, we shall all be brothers and rise together to meet God, our wonderful Creator.

Such great joy will this be, and I am now confident in everyone I meet that he or she is sent by you, God, to help me fulfill my role in Your grand plan.

What God has ordained for us here and now,

Rather than upon what we don't have, though we might want more.

WHEN IN ROME

WHEN IN ROME, DO AS THE ROMANS DO.

"When in Rome, do as the Romans do!" Didn't we all hear this expression as children? Now to apply it to our world. We had the Nazis, for instance, though not for very long. For at least sixteen years, they flourished. So if you were born there and presumed to be an Aryan, then it was compulsory to "hail Caesar" like the gladiators with your arm held straight and fingers held tightly together or to go off to Dachau, an extermination camp.

Of course now we have Trump in America, who wants to make America great again. Some people say America has always been great and that a narcistic toddler-in-chief is no remedy at all. It is really a personal choice to stand up against evil.

I have told my few followers to greet all their friends as though each and every friend is a "saint sent from heaven," which is not always the case. So I apologize for my error and add that you yourself are the potential true saint in such cases where others are less than saintly. It is up to you to help guide all lost souls into the kingdom of heaven by your kindness. When they hate you, Jesus said, be glad, because all the saints and prophets have been hated and persecuted before you. A place in heaven is opening up for you.

When you are kind and offer others the shirt off your back or a coat or condolences, then heaven is descending to the earth and the "kingdom of heaven" is here and now, like a ray of sunlight on this dark planet.

Be hopeful then that you can make a difference. You who are reborn in God are also kind to others and animals. We are all God's children, and all of us deserve love; it is the glue of life that keeps us alive and hopeful.

I beseech you to consider St. Mohammed when traveling in Arabia or mingling with Muslims; consider that they know what love is and what friendship is. Their St. Mohammed banned alcohol and espoused cleanliness in an effort to bring all his followers to worship one God.

My roommate at Holderness spread out his prayer shawl on the floor of our small room and kneeled and then bowed low in his observance of "the Faith." It is very good for the thyroid gland, which operates on gravity to tip upside down to cleanse itself. I am not a doctor, so I don't know this for a fact. But I do know, in yoga, which has been practiced for thousands of years, the devotees, called yogis, assume many positions to express their devotion.

When in Asia, do as the Asians do. You can emulate your friends and not be entirely different from them. Thereby they might feel less threatened for being who they are.

Of course, if they are evil or self-destructive, there is no benefit in emulating darkness and ignorance.

You are full of the knowledge that God loves us all equally. It is we who choose whether to receive all this free love from our Creator, who gives us life.

MURDER BY ALCOHOL

THE MILLARS ARE AT IT AGAIN. THIS AFTER THEY'D AGREED TO PET SIT MY dog Nita and abandoning her at their home during long summer drives in my car. I was in South America skiing (it was winter down there), and they'd take their own dog Chas with them, returning home late.

"Oh, Nita broke all the screen windows trying to escape from the second story."

Tricky Dicky Boone had bought them the house with his near-perfect truck driving credit. The Millars managed to get themselves on the deed as owners in common or whatever it's called. However, they were living upstairs in the attic, which was just fine during the ice-cold first winter.

Unfortunately, summer came with the baby still crying, and Duncan fell off the wagon again, or the bus so to speak. He was popping the aluminum beer can tops by ten thirty every morning after going cold turkey for forty days and nights. He had seen Odin in Valhalla instead of Elijah and the burning bush. This happens often to beer league ski racers. They attend after-ski race parties all winter long at posh nearby winter tourist resorts called "ski areas." So the sign on the highway says. And it points in the direction of the rich and affluent, who have nothing better to do all winter long in New Hampshire but go skiing—a sport that includes the base lodge activities of "hot chocolate" and then gossip and then probably spike the hot chocolate with schnapps and then French kiss your girlfriend in the snowbank while your wife is waiting for you in the car and so on.

At any rate. Millar fell off the wagon again, as it is now was the beginning of summer year two in the new old house with broken screen windows.

Ring, ring, ring went the phone again. And it was Millar wanting new screen windows for the old house worth $250k, double my own. But me being a skier, my father had bought mine when I turned sixty-two, retirement age, as his own father had bought his for him when he'd returned alive from World War II.

"Your bookkeeper for the family, Jim, says all you have to do is sign the paper, and he'll send the money to Lowes for our new screen windows—twelve in all. And god darn it, why can't you?"

"My father is dead and gone to Albany" (a town with no people in Vermont), "so there's no more money coming in. His third wife got most of it, and his second wife's children are still suing him for art treasures their mother bought with his money. Get over it!" *Clang.* I hang up the phone.

On my laptop, I order from Amazon three screen repair patch kits. It would be cheaper just to go to the liquor store myself and buy three bottles of tequila and one of schnapps to help them make another screaming baby. The first one has stopped screaming by now, and so they are resuming screaming at me.

"You ruined our lives!"

I did? I think there was some interplay, as they tried to ruin mine by calling the police when I brought home a new girlfriend from Rhode Island. Good thing I had not brought my second wife home from Colorado. She drinks like a fish or did at the time of our marriage. Usually at least one person in every marriage drinks, to mold into it better as a sort of compromise?

"Listen, you Millars, you have a new house and a new life not under my roof anymore—as you finally moved out taking all my possessions with you to go live with Dick Boone happily ever after as he has whole cases of Seagram's 7. Be happy!"

Now they want window screen credit at Lowe's of about $500 or more, when they probably have window screen patch kits, so the vast majority of the money is going to some other project—in other words, the liquor store.

In America, they almost passed assisted suicide so doctors could kill their patients before bankrupting them. The banks would have no such thing and put a stop to that. The national pastime is still "murder by alcohol," which is the prevalent form of manslaughter nationwide. If you don't like your spouse, take him or her to the bar and then call a cab for yourself because you have decided to go feed the cat at home.

Dick Boone, your days are numbered living with those Millars. They will want your downstairs bedroom. And if you die, the whole house belongs to them.

Why don't you have a wife, Mr. Boone? Well, we can just guess the answer to that one, as you must love those Millars—at least it appears so.

Consider the outcome of this soap opera in America, which plays every afternoon all day into each and every evening.

Ring, ring, ring! "It's the Millar's calling again!" says my new girlfriend, now wife.

"Hang up and call the police. No just call down to the liquor store! Tell them the Millars and Mr. Boone can have anything they want!"

Problem solved the American way.

THE DROUGHT

THE HORSES HAVE BEEN LET OUT OF THE BARN WITH JOHN BOLTON'S NEW book, which has been released in spite of the Trump administration's attempt to block its publication.

There is a severe drought in several states that will not go away until the present administration leaves office. The American public thinks that greed is a virtue, and capitalism—unchecked and unbalanced, with no restraint—is the very will of God, who will, by divine grace, intercede in this pandemic and global warming and put the brakes on both.

The drought continues. The polar ice caps and world's glaciers are in retreat. At the Trump rally in Tulsa, Oklahoma, six staff workers have tested positive for Corona virus and won't be admitted.

God's judgment of the vile human race is approaching with lightning speed.

The planet, Mother Earth, will defend herself with hurricanes, droughts, floods, earthquakes, and the World Health Organization which would like to help the poor but has been defunded, like the police.

So shall there be any remedy to this while the rich get richer and thrive at the expense of everyone else, including future generations?

We are urging our own neighbors to stop cutting the brown grass so short, as it is just one more factor contributing to the aridity.

VISIONS OF THE GREEN PRINCE (OF LUND) ON MIDSUMMER NIGHT: GREEN LEAVES BLOOMING

Visions of the Green Prince who sees green leaves blooming

The long night of human madness
Must end, or man will perish.
So now must come the dawn of human awakening.

The system of greed and pollution must be compromised,
Or the planet will become something we no longer recognize as our own
Since we will not even exist.

While traveling abroad, I have been reborn in spirit
At the prospect of world green revolution.

Because corporate greed
Is destroying our way of a healthy lifestyle,

The USA has become the sickest dog
In the pack of hounds running wildly.

People are encouraged there
Not to walk or bicycle but to drive fast luxury cars
To Walmart, where they park in handicap parking and
Ride electric wheelchairs through the endless aisles
Because they have lost the use of their feet.

This lifestyle of heart attack, stroke, and cancer
Must be averted by the followers and proponents of the Green
Revolution;

And this mindless architecture of misadventure needs be taken back to
the drawing board and recreated by
Proponents of Life not Death!

So what needs to be done is for the people to seize their governments,
Take control of their governments,
Be responsible for themselves.

This will not be an easy task.
Individually, we cannot accomplish much politically.
We will need to create a worldwide party in this endeavor.

Each of us was once lost in the darkness of material consumption;
From this, we fell ill,
Became depressed and burdened
By anxiety.

But now we see the light.
It is bright and shining
Like the sun.
We will raise high our Green Standards (Banners).
This world is not just for corporate CEOs.
It is our world too;
We must take it back!

There is a green Prince or Princess in each and every one of us.
We must look inside ourselves
To find the strength to rid ourselves and the planet
Of this corporate plague.

We must have government of the people
For the people.

So help us God that we as a Green Nation of the living
Do not perish in a perishing world,
Because Life is essential to us.
Therefore raise high your Green Banner of Truth and the Way.
Be of clean conscience and be cleansed
There are people like Bernie Sanders, whom we endorse.
He is a prophet
Before his time;
So are We.

The proponents of Big Business do not like to hear
What we have to say
Because the Gargantuan Hospitals
Will go broke without patients.

Here at the Lund Train Station,
There are three thousand bicycles.
So this might be considered
The capitol of something very good brewing.

The Wind is shifting in Our Direction.
And like brave Vikings
We shall all raise Our green Mast and Sail.
God be with Us and against those who destroy the Planet!

After all, Our Health is more important than wealth.

DEATH OF PEG

PEG LAY DYING IN HER BED AT CAMP TAMARACK IN THE NEWLY constructed one-bedroom house. Most of the family was there off and on, except for the grandchildren, who just passed by quickly to say they were on their way to activities somewhere.

I wasn't really a part of the family, as I only cut the grass. Peg hadn't wanted to pay me cash for that activity, so I ended up working for her sons building tennis courts at New England Tennis Court Company. We drove those two-ton and three-ton trucks everywhere but Rhode Island—which meant Maine, Vermont, Massachusetts, even Connecticut once. I remember getting up at four one morning, and we nailed down tapes close to midnight. I got four hours of sleep that night. As for overtime pay we didn't get that either.

The Kenneys were Scotch and German on Peg's side of the family and thrifty, whereas her husband, Jack, was half Irish and half English nobility. In fact, one of the ancestors was John Wilkes Booth's Yankee girlfriend. Enough said of that, the Kenneys were honest people, as Jack had attended Dartmouth and been a New England tennis champion and held other titles. Before that, Jack had been a messenger "runner" on one of those destroyers in the Battle of Midway, which was the turning point of the war in the Pacific, 1942, though that was five years before I was born.

Peg had always wanted to be a ski racer, as she had grown up in flat Leavenworth, Kansas, which is an army barracks, including a very morbid-looking Leavenworth Military Prison. She definitely wanted to leave that place behind, and her military father too. She met Jack, a

Dartmouth student, in New England, and it was love at first sight. Jack borrowed some money and bought a thousand-acre farm in Easton, New Hampshire, just over the Franconia line near where Robert Frost wrote his famous poem, "Two Paths Diverged in a Yellow Wood." And I took the same path, ending up in Easton Valley myself cutting grass.

Peg had a very flirtatious, attractive daughter who wore tartan kilts upon occasion. And she had a lot of very white Anglo-Saxon friends, as that was the entire nearby population on Sugar Hill.

"Cook me some soup, please, Duncan," Peg commanded me from her deathbed.

I complied immediately, as she was camp commander.

Jack was the camp comedian but had recently developed Alzheimer's and had been shipped out to VA Hospital in Tilton for wetting his diapers and forgetting to change them. Jack had been writing his memoirs, which were over a thousand pages, as he didn't want to forget anything but sensed that was the developing problem. We all missed Jack and his humor, and his kids took long trips down to Tilton to see him but not Peg. She went bicycling up to two weeks before her death of that cancer.

I fumbled nervously, opened the can of chicken soup, and boiled it and then brought it to Peg's bedside table.

"This soup has no taste!" said Peg, complaining.

So her daughter took it back over to the stove and added some herbs, salt, and pepper.

There were some things I never told Peg, like almost everything, as we kids back then wanted to drink beer, chase girls, and smoke pot if someone had any. The Beatles, a rock group selling records off the charts, encouraged everybody to take LSD and go wild.

I was lying on the table in Argentina where they tortured people. They had broken my nose, and blood had been gushing out like a river. I had never experienced that. Then they broke my jaw. I had never experienced that either. Otto Skorzeny was in charge of the interrogation, as he wanted to learn more about Portillo Ski Hotel in Chile and what was transpiring three weeks prior to my capture. There was a meeting in the back of the hotel near the employees' living quarters.

Allende, a Communist, was running for president in the Chilean election. And if he won, he was going to give Portillo Hotel to its most minor shareholder, a leftist who had invited some Israeli Communists to be his guests, and use it as a base to attack "Nazi" Argentina in Bariloche with the purpose of kidnapping (or killing) Dr. Josef Mengele and maybe even Otto Skorzeny if possible. Otto had, just a year before, blown up a building in Buenos Aires with five hundred employees arriving for work just twenty minutes prior. It had been home of *Soviet Life* and other Marxist Russian propaganda magazines and a left-wing newspaper or two, *Pravda* and *Proletariat Gauchos Arise* or something akin.

I had been invited to attend that informal meeting by some young Israelis, who asked for my cooperation in hunting down a Nazi war criminal by being a spotter on the inside in Bariloche, to which I had been invited to ski race. I was only sixteen years old, and I didn't realize that constituted espionage, punishable by death. It all seemed like fun and games to me, still a child mentally, so to speak.

I was faking being unconscious, as I didn't want to be beaten further—worse than any dog. Otto was talking with someone, maybe Hans Rudel, the pilot who had invited me to the ski races.

"I am just tired of killing children. It seems like there is an endless parade of them sent here by God to avenge their losses in the war. I am just tired of killing. Why don't you kill him yourself? Everybody wants me to do the killing. I am tired. Get him up and I will ask him some more questions," he ordered.

They hit me again. That was the only question they had and added the answer.

"You are going to die, so tell us everything. You are not leaving this place!"

I had never told anyone but my psychiatrist under sodium pentothal about any of these dismal atrocities. I wanted to forget them. But everything that had happened to me in Argentina still showed in my self-esteem, which amounted to none at all. I had a lot of doubts about everything in general.

I was upset that my soup was rejected, and it was time to leave. It was the last time I saw Peg. She died two days later.

"Peg was a revolutionary ahead of her time." I spoke at the memorial service for her.

Bob and Pam Fisher were there from Conway, plus three hundred people. I meant to say that Peg was a daughter of the American Revolution. She died before her grandson Bode Miller had even won one of his five Olympic ski medals.

He was on the crew building tennis courts starting about age seven. I told him ski stories during the lunch and coffee breaks of the work crew. Working very young, he developed a work ethic, but it drowned out his creative playfulness. Everything was work to him and serious at that. He wanted more for himself than to build tennis courts his whole life. Everybody drank beer after work, and Bode got a few sips and developed a taste for it way back then.

THE WOOING
OF CRISTINA

GARY GRABBED HIS FIANCÉE'S SMALL DOG BY THE NECK AND THEN HELD it outside the window of the pickup from the passenger side while the driver pulled his pistol and cocked it at Gary's temple, threatening to shoot. The fiancée of possibly both of them simultaneously, sitting in the middle, let out a death-defying scream at the sight of her mini poodle held by its neck outside the truck window at sixty miles per hour as the truck made a tight turn above a five hundred-foot cliff.

Needless to say, the engagement was called off almost immediately, with the young woman dialing 9-1-1. A Telluride police officer arrived and put Gary in handcuffs. He was bailed out and sitting at the bar when I met him.

He began smiling and telling me about his recent engagement.

"I don't know what I'll do with this sixteen-carat diamond engagement ring," he confessed to me.

Upon close inspection, I decided to offer him half the price he had paid for it—approximately $400.

There was a young lady I had met on the Nastar town racing hill. She was the "starter" and collected race fees for the Telluride Ski Company. I had been fired the year before as a six-year ski instructor for Telluride Company there in the Colorado Rockies. I had no ski pass and climbed up the ski trails daily to race either Nastar or the biweekly beer league Challenge Cup.

Cristina was the name of my favorite employee. She was always reading books, with nothing else better to do unless a swarm of ski racers suddenly showed up to race. Then they were soon racing off and gone. She put their money and signed liability releases in a company purse. Then back to her dime novel she would go. I imagine she read romance novels, not calculus or philosophy. She was a very pleasant young lady, fresh out of college from Rhode Island, supporting her never-present boyfriend, who went fishing or ice climbing.

I finally asked her the big question. "If I can guess when you were born, will you love me forever?" It was a bit more complicated than that, though I cannot seem to recall the part two. But I do remember the answer to part one was, "You were born on your birthday, silly!"

Many Telluride romances had even shorter conversations than ours. And the view of Mount Wilson and twenty other snow-capped peaks surrounded by sun, moon, and stars probably had more to do with bringing young couples together than even words could express. When the fruit on the tree is ripe, so they say.

Sometimes words were less important than mugs of cold beer with a tequila chaser on Telluride nights. Then young knights would sit in the Last Dollar Saloon with their peaking, decked-out damsels, warming up for a full night of fine food and fornication.

I suppose I wanted even more than that from my every Telluride romance, as I told Cristina I was leaving town very soon, but I had a friendship ring to give her. This I said while I stood in her starting gate, maybe for the very last time, as spring was arriving now, and the ski area would close soon.

"Really?" She was curious at the taped friendship ring I put on her finger before leaving the starting gate. She was inquisitive like a cat.

"Oh it's so beautiful," she said. "But I can't marry you. I have a man friend already. I will have to give it back!"

She did marry him after all, and they moved back to Stowe, Vermont, where his family was from. They raised two children and lived happily ever after.

Gary wrote me a postcard from British Honduras, which said, "I finally inherited a lot of money and came here. Too bad you are not one of the beautiful people, or I would have invited you to come along."

MY HORSE

Oh this sick, plastic gasoline world is self-destructing.

I just want to climb on my horse and ride

Across the endless steppes like Attila the Hun.

At least I would have one friend, my horse!

Because my car is actually no friend at all, just a machine.

Its windows enclose and segregate me from the earth

And deprive me of many friends I would better meet while walking on foot;

Also it burns gasoline, and this is wrecking my environment.

While my horse farts methane gas, still this is far less injurious than Donald Trump.

Why are our leaders in denial? Perhaps they all have so little time left here on earth

They just don't care about future generations, which it seems now will be mostly insects,

Our entire way of life is in peril—we are on the very edge of extinction.

What can I do about all this? Maybe my horse knows?

So I will get high on my horse and ride and see a different view of this earth and steppe.

I will look toward a new beginning for modern man in an environmentally safe ecosystem.

So much has to change right now, and it all begins

With me and my horse.

I AM THE NEW GERMANY

My father and his mistress and her son my own age hurry through

The crowded rush-hour streets of Dusseldorf, Germany.

She let go of my hand. They hurried off. I didn't keep up. In 1956,

I was eight years old and lost wandering in the bombed-out ruins,

A neighborhood destroyed by the Second World War's Allied bombing raids—

Searchlights in the sky, antiaircraft guns firing projectiles and tracer bullets from machine guns, illuminating shadows of bombers fleeing, crashing, burning.

Now the sun shines through haze cement mixers all spinning fresh mortar,

The happy masons all smiling at me, even some tough women laying bricks.

"Are you lost? We can call a policeman."

I am young and happy to have so many new friends. Some are children pointing at me or shaking my hand.

This must be heaven here—the New Germany rising from ashes.

There are locomotives steaming along the Rhine River.

Switzerland is not too very far away, with cows and cheese and more smiling people.

Everyone is so happy that the war is over and no more Hitler.

He tried to do so many things for the German people;

Oh what a mess that became. Germany was invaded.

All the fathers and grandfathers went off to Russia never to return.

The Russians are cannibals and maybe ate them; who knows?

The United States is our ally and loans us money to buy all this cement.

France still has the Eiffel Tower and that big main street with all the cars racing for the lead whenever the stoplight changes.

Hitler killed himself, and all his henchmen were arrested and brought to trial.

Now the sun is shining again, and there is hope, the long nightmare ended.

"I am the New Germany. Where is your father? Are you American, little comrade?" asks a boy my size.

"He is one of us now. Ha, ha, ha" says another.

Finally a policeman comes and asks me my name.

"I am Kullmann Dunkin." This makes the policeman smile.

We walk off toward the police station.

I would have much rather stayed

I would have much rather stayed

Among the poor and joyous people.

They had lost everything but found God.

They had lived in tents under blankets and tarps.

Now they were happy at last.

Now they were happy!

WHAT WOULD I
TELL YOU IF I WERE
YOUR PRESIDENT?

What would I say to you if

I were George Washington or Abraham Lincoln,

Now that we are in a pandemic and if I were your president? Hmm.

"My fellow Americans,

"I am dearly sorry for this great misfortune, which is upon us like a plague

"There were much better times of great prosperity at least for some of us

"Before this unprecedented catastrophe struck us,

"Leaving endless semitrucks with frozen bodies of so many dead

"Stacked upon one another. Now they are lost to us forever,

"But they have found a new home with God their Creator

"Let us remember their great love and the sacrifice they made to their families to sustain all God's children, who we are;

"Let their deaths not be in vain, nor our own, because we are all mortal.

"God may call us each home at the time of His choosing.

"We must prepare ourselves for that calling by being good Samaritans now,

"By our vigilance and sacrifice in this life and in this time of need.

"We are required to ask what we can do for our country and each other

"Because we are all in this together, in a struggle, locked together in this struggle to overcome great adversity.

"This is a great trial against a common enemy, and we must prevail or perish.

"So imagine personally what each one of us can do best and put us to work to be divine;

"Give us tasks to perform that we might align better with heaven and righteousness,

"That we realize we are all a band of brothers in an army of one to perform with a common goal of victory,

"Like soldiers in an army of God predestined to win the very good fight

"Because we are neither slothful nor lazy.

"We know, yes, we realize this is our destiny to be in this war against a virus and against disease and ignorance and darkness.

"The truth will come to light, and we will know that adversity has refined us like pure gold in a fire.

"In this sea of tempest, in this ravaging storm thrown upon us,

"We will point our bow into the wind

"Or do whatever else might be best to sail out of this passing storm cast upon us now.

"There will be better days ahead, and a better world with God awaits us all.

"This is but our test to endure and be refined and made pure and true as by love itself."

(I won't want the job unless, of course, we might all love each other. But in politics, that is not too likely.)

ONE MORE DAY TO

So glad am I that I have one more day

To rise up and shine forth like the sun; will I be kind?

This is the day that God has made

Actors salesmen, firemen, and police.

If you are not criminal, you have no reason to hide nor to lie.

Go forward, obeying the laws and commandments.

Sing a joyous song and be glad; you who live give thanks.

Seek all who are hidden in fear and cowardice

Because Jesus came to save sinners, not the righteous.

You who aspire to be saintly, befriend everyone you meet.

Distribute the good news that God will surely forgive them who repent
and believe;

God has died for their sins that they might be saved and not die,

God who has made this wondrous day, the day of our salvation.

The long shadows of doubt will have fled away

On this day when sinners shall reform

Because of the love that is given to them

By God, through his many saints everywhere.

So do not ask the color of the skin of God's people.

They are of every color and creed, every religion and every sexual identity,

Every political persuasion operating 24/7 in every corner of the universe.

Our God is the Lord of hosts, who manifests all creation.

Praise God; for every little thing be thankful.

HAPPY AND UNHAPPY CAMPERS AT SUMMER CAMP

I thought, perhaps erroneously, that you might find rest by retiring early,

As the sun is now setting in the West, but you are grief-stricken.

You are full of sorrow that has turned to anger because black lives do matter.

Therefore, you are still in the streets, marching tonight in every major city, even my own, Littleton, a tiny hamlet.

Perhaps if you were back in school, you would have homework;

Or if it was not a pandemic, you would be playing baseball or working in a restaurant for tips.

Now in this new normal, with no job and no money, you are frustrated and hungry.

Also, with no home to go to, the curfews make no sense at all,

You are living in the streets, so *you are home*!

And this very thick president, who cares more about his political base than his country, threatens you

To push the very last of your buttons, whereby you will totally lose it—your rational behavior.

I wrongly assumed that you protestors had homes to go to.

If you were right-wingers, you could go home to right-wing parents,

Where you would be fed their ideologies at the dinner table—

That black people are inferior and just ignore them, just forget them.

You were taught at school that all men are born equal and to love one another,

Yet at the dinner table, the very rich will explain this is impractical,

That aristocrats beget aristocratic children, and servants come from parents who were servants.

Our wonderful America is a country of rich and poor, and now with coronavirus,

There will be no summer camp at all for the poor, no backgammon, no croquet,

No tennis, no horseback riding, no swimming, no canoeing, no nothing.

The poor of all this world have become poorer, and the rich, richer.

You can see all this on television, that there are products that many people simply cannot afford—

Boats, planes, cars, trucks, motor homes, chalets, houses, second homes, condominiums.

Now, about a job—well, normally it's a favor to your parents that someone might even hire you in the first place.

Since you have no parents, you can clean the latrines or be a bedpan nurse.

So hopefully, my summer campers, your parents are rich, because that is the American dream.

For everyone else, it's an American nightmare. But you won't hear about it in books because poor people cannot afford to write them.

Nightmare books are not exactly best sellers, but American success stories are popular and selling well.

This essay is to inform you that you, the reader, are very fortunate indeed

To gain this insight into class warfare that threatens to divide our country, as well as other countries.

The public education system of our country is the only bridge to ensure that no child gets left behind.

With this pandemic, everyone is getting left behind. We have deboarded our national bus.

The bus of our nation has had two flat tires, with only one spare tire.

We have just broken down, and by looting and burning our cities, we are reentering the Stone Age.

So please try to remember just which book it was you were reading before this pandemic hit.

Our president is holding a Bible, which he has obviously never read nor understood.

We cannot each of us be experts in every field, as we have just so many brain cells.

Try to use the ones that God has given you and imagine a better world.

Have hope and courage and love, plus faith, and we will all get through this together.

ST. GEORGE FLOYD AND ALL THE SAINTS

St. George Floyd,

He was an evangelist and a Christian.

He was a big brother to many and said,

"You can go up or you can go down."

So let us choose for ourselves which path we take.

What he wanted for us was not violence, which begets more violence.

His life and premature death is worth protesting.

The streets are full in every major city.

Many others have died due to police brutality;

Profiling, whether about race, religion, sexual orientation, or politics,

Is injustice pure and simple.

Let my people go.

Let my people out of Egypt and slavery.

Let my people be free.

Let my people enter the Promised Land of salvation.

God himself shall wipe away their tears.

They will walk in the Promised Land.

They will enter the garden of Eden.

They will find peace and glory

On that Day of Justice, on that Day of the Lord,

We will sing hallelujah.

LIGHTS OUT

Happy or unhappy, my favorite little campers,

It's time for bed and lights out.

Tomorrow is a new day. There will be a morning inspection.

Be sure to make your beds with hospital corners.

The camp commander is coming to your room personally.

Have your house in order and respectfully stand at attention.

Pay homage, and lip service if need be, to those who guide you in this life.

Respect and cherish those who love you and bring you to camp.

There may be some of you who will just run off into the forest to live with wolves or up in trees like the monkeys,

I cannot predict who will stand with us in this holy war to restore the peace.

It requires discipline to be a soldier and love to be a disciple.

So you who have ears, listen up, because God loves you and wants you to be safe.

God is concerned for your safety and will protect you.

You are running around with lit fuses ready to explode; God will defuse you

From burning down your own house, before you hurt your favorite neighbor,

Before you see your best friend die or some innocent old lady.

Come home to those who love you; surely the police do not.

I am giving you this one last chance to turn your life around.

You must work within the system to change it.

You must pray for justice, because God has ears and is not deaf,

And justice will come rolling down like a river breaking over its banks.

Evil cannot last while God always triumphs in the end.

Life is good, and that is the lesson for you happy campers tonight.

FWD: DOG STORY (CONT.) GOV. PERRY IS A RELATIVE, AS MY BIRTH FATHER WAS AN ALABAMA MINISTER PERRY ALSO, AND WE ALL KNOW I'M OUT THERE

Date: Wed, Aug 10, 2011 at 8:09 a.m.
Written by the dog JP

I WAS A VERY FAST RUNNER IN MY YOUTH. I THEN HAD TWENTY-SEVEN PUPPY descendants and grandpuppies. I was the pack leader of quite a large pack of sleekish hounds, numbering usually between five and twelve—all of us in that pickup truck, yes. Those were the days of my youth.

My sons names were Oscar Mayer Wienermeister; Roofer; Spotted Scotty; Tiny Thing, who was born a bit small; Houdini; and Becko and Andreo. And my daughters were Maykala and Construction Girl. I even ended up with some of my sisters from my birth litter, Sara and Katarina, and, yes, a brother, Roberto, who barked a lot and was given away at Bretton Woods Ski Area to an Irish-looking family with eager Irish-looking children. But he, Roberto, was run over by a car, I heard. How tragic!

Although I usually ran in a pack, my owner usually followed us all in his pickup truck. Mostly, we ran along the edges of those side roads, and more often when no other cars were on those roads. Occasionally, we might see a cat and chase it to its home. But we never actually caught one until—Silverton.

Yes, this happened once upon a historic time in Silverton, Colorado, at 9,333 feet above sea level, in less than ten degrees above zero, and during a raging snowstorm, a whiteout blizzard. Perhaps it was November. I am not very good with dates. Well, Sara had just had another fresh batch of puppies, who she was guarding while out street walking. And suddenly she smelled a wildcat in her midst in the snowstorm, and her doggy instincts were unable to decipher whether it was a housecat or a mountain lion. She was still swollen in her teats from breastfeeding her young puppies.

Well, to make a long story short, she assumed the worst-case scenario and killed it dead, snapping its neck in the snow-covered street. The cat owners found their dearly beloved tabby deceased, stiff and frozen in the snowbank the very next morning early.

There was an immediate investigation, which ended up in my owner being summoned into court. The impending fines for eight loose dogs unchained was almost nine hundred dollars. The judge, I heard, looked very stern and mean, as the owners of the deceased tabby were his neighbors.

My owner sat there in the courtroom with his newly married second wife, a lesbian, and her girlfriend. "Your Honor," pleaded my owner, "Sara, as a protective mother of newborn, could not ascertain whether the feline was domestic or of the wilderness, wild, and reacted instinctively as any mother in the face of grave danger!"

The fine was reduced somewhat.

As a result of this atrocity and fracas, now, cats in Silverton, Colorado, are required by law to be leashed when off their owners' properties in the downtown area or when strolling away from home. It is perhaps the only place in the entire world where all tabbies and other house cats are required to be leashed so as to be recognized as domestic animals, with pertinent rights of protection by law—all because of my sister Sara.

JEAN CLAUDE KILLY
AND HONORE BONNET

SKI WEDELN, THE AUSTRIAN SKI TECHNIQUE BY DR. KRUCKENHAUSER AND his protégé, my ski coach Dr Clemens "Miki" Hutter, was published in 1960 in several languages, at a time when Austrian skiers were winning all the major competitions, including the Olympics. Names like Othmar Schneider, Anderl Molterer, Pepi Steigler, Ernst Hinterseer, Egon Zimmerman, and Karl Schranz were in the European news daily.

There had been a famous French skier, Emile Allais, and the young Norwegian, Stein Erikson. But the Austrians soon took over and won everything. Until along came another Frenchman, Guy Perrilat; a compact dynamo at only five foot three, he was fearless and won several big European downhills in 1961. The French government took notice of its talented young skiers and drafted many into the French Postal Service and the army.

When, in 1958, the French colony Algeria revolted, many young Frenchmen were sent there to serve, including two aspiring ski racers, Jean Claude Killy and Michel Arpin, who got shot in the ass. However, both lived and returned to the French Alps, where Honore Bonet was organizing a very large contingency. It included Francois Bonlieu, whose parents had, in the French underground in World War II, been shot in front of his eyes. Also involved were Perrillat and Killy, Arpin, Leo Lacroix, Georges Mauduit, Alain Penz, Patrick Russell, and many more.

Suddenly, the Austrians were to dominate no more, as France produced superior skis of a new design—Rossignol, Dynamic, and Dynastar, all wrapped in fiberglass. And Jean Claude Killy won eleven World Cup victories in a row, including three at Cannon Mountain, New Hampshire, and then three Olympic medals in Grenoble, 1968. This equaled the three gold medals won by Austrian Toni Sailer in 1956. But Toni Sailer had been an upset there in Cortina because his teammate Anderl Molterer had won all the races leading up to those Olympics. No one has ever done this—up to modern times.

Then Bob Beattie and Benson Hedges of New York brought Killy out of semiretirement to race "professionally" (he had already accumulated $1 million) in North America's World Pro Skiing. With televised ski competitions in a dual format, racers would go head-to-head over jumps built into the racecourses. Sponsors were found, and money spent in advertising. The ski industry, which had relocated somewhat to Boulder, Colorado, was on a roll with Head, Hart, and K2 skis and Lange boots made in America.

Then came the economic slowdown of 1975 to 1981, and many businesses moved to Italy for cheaper labor. Alpine pro Skiing on US soil never recovered.

Spyder Sabich, who emerged as the great American hope to fend off the European dominance, was shot and killed mistakenly (?) by his lover, Claudine Longet. Apparently it was an accident, she claimed, although her illegally confiscated diary claimed to the contrary. Christmas singer Andy Williams's wife. Then the Palmer brothers, Terry and Tyler; Ken Corrock; and Hank Kashiwa attempted to replace the mystic of the legendary Spider. The latter had been the son of a Serbian American sheriff of Kyburz, California. But pro ski racing slid off the charts, as suddenly, there came ballet skiing and then hotdog and acrobatic skiing with Suzy Chaffee, a former downhill racer, and Wayne Wong.

Before it was all said and done, I managed to beat Killy once in a celebrity race, causing his team, including Ethel Kennedy, to suffer second place. Then, while I was racing Killy at Hunter Mountain, his ski came off; he hit the snow, falling first before I fell. So technically I was the winner of that heat.

But Beattie overruled course referee Lasse Hamre and declared, "Killy advances to the next round, not Cullman. Killy was slightly ahead."

In another race, I managed third at Hunter Mountain, losing to great Austrian World Cup skier Hugo Nindl and then his sidekick, Harold Steufer, who had eyes on my girlfriend, Diane. Oh well, I had my fun. I even managed some conversation with Michele Arpin and Alain Penz, as they spoke broken English. But my French was nonexistent; thus, I never managed a word with Killy. As for Spider Sabich, we hated each other, understandably.

CAMPFIRE AND GUITAR

Having departed from my father,

Who had taken me to an institution for the sick

With my new stepmother, they then abandoned me there

In the region of so many godless psychiatrists,

I had traveled to Argentina only to be tortured there—

Tortured for winning a ski race and confessing

I had met some Israelis in Portillo who were hatching a plot to capture Mengele.

My own girlfriend, who I had met there, was also Jewish.

Her father had survived Auschwitz, though her mother was Chilean and Spanish.

She said I should do it for her people—go there to Argentina and be a lookout,

Be a spy and participate on the side of good.

"Just what was in it for you? Money?" asked my father.

"You should have considered how you would benefit yourself!"

(There are so many war heroes, all broken and homeless!)

We have but one father, but soon, I would have two or three.

Soon I would wander in northern New Hampshire on my bicycle

From family to family, the life of a bard or poet.

With a guitar, I would have sung a sweeter, more melodious ballad.

Then, I might have been forgiven. Then, I might have forgiven myself

With success and snorted cocaine with so many rich, affluent people.

Surely my life had been one of self-destruction

Because my own father abandoned me to the wolves; surely, my bad decisions

He would not forgive them for fifty years; finally he did;

When it would be too late for me to return to my heavenly Father, I did.

So it is never too late, but if I look back

It is like a battlefield in a sea of destruction. I must look forward instead.

I have my new guitar now finally. I sing my song at the campfire.

You are here to comfort me; you are here to let me love myself as well.

NONA OKUN, MENGELE'S GIRLFRIEND SENT TO ME BY GOD FOR TRUTH AND JUSTICE

I N 1965, I WAS IN SOUTH STATION ALMOST EVERY WEEKEND FROM CHRISTMAS until March. The reason was that I was recovering from trauma inflicted by those desperate agents of evil, the men in black. The one who jumped upon the stage in the café was none other than the Angel of Death himself, Josef Mengele. He had actually been with ski troops in support of a Panzer division sent to break through with supplies for the German forces of Von Paulus surrounded by soviets in Stalingrad. When one of the tanks was hit, Mengele jumped upon its turret and pulled two burning *kameraden* from it, saving their lives. For this, he received medals of bravery and loyalty to the Führer Adolf Hitler. Und Hitler ist Deutschland, und Deutschland ist Adolf Hitler, and so on.

So Mengele went to the hospital back in Germany with burns and a broken ankle from his adventure. His professor contacted him with utmost authority to ensure a promotion for him should he accept a command at Auschwitz, a prison of war camp and much worse as history would reveal.

Mengele went there after his recovery, and because he had authority to save so many people for experimentation, he also saved a tall, young white Russian woman, whose real name I am unsure of, but her Israeli passport later gave her the name Mona Nishkin or something similar. Because she was like a girlfriend to him, he saved her and then hid her. She survived the war to go to New York and South America, where she claimed to me she had recently seen her captor, "the Angel of Death" himself, wandering around Oliva, a suburb of Buenos Aires. Of course she insisted that I could help them (Israelis?) track him down because he was wanted for war crimes. I felt somewhat willing, as it seemed adventurous!

So she insisted that, at the end of my every ski run, I should slow down and wait for the man on one ski with one leg, who was constantly trying to catch up with me, as he would probably offer to take me over the border to ski in Argentina. I was gullible and naive, my father later explained to me, because they offered me nothing in return for a great deal. I never should have listened to her or them.

Water under a bridge now, because I went to Argentina, where the pilot insisted I take a room with the Syrian refugees from the war. Of course, I had been part of that great meeting in the back servants' quarters of Hotel Portillo, where communists and subversives made plans for any left-wing cause. But I was told to leave the meeting early because, if I were captured, it would be better the less I knew.

So there in the Syrian auchluss escape house for all refugees from the war (on the losing Nazi side), I unpacked my things amid a heavy downpour. Suddenly, one of the Israelis who had been camping demanded space on my floor. He insisted, pointing his Berretta in my face.

The Nazis had eyes and ears everywhere and knew I had been visited by a subversive. So already I was a marked man boy, and it would just be a short time before Rudel escorted me in his stainless silver 1953 Porsche to Skorzeny for questioning Argentine style.

They ask you the question, and then before you can answer, they just hit you anyway, blood splattering everywhere. No fun at all, not even for a teenager. My jaw was broken; I couldn't talk anyway. And then they decided to dislocate my right hip just for fun so I couldn't walk.

Thrown into a jail cell, I presumed I had been left there to die, when suddenly, they brought one of the Israeli campers, who they had caught dozing in the rain-soaked puma pampa.

They came to take him to interrogation, asking him just who he was, and he replied to those men in black. "I am Jesus Christ, sent to redeem your lost souls, in fact, to save you from death and grant you eternal life."

He was so very funny I almost laughed, but then they shot him in a place where the wound was indeed mortal. And he slowly began to die in the jail cell with me. Luckily, just prior to this, he had put my hip back in its socket, so I was beginning to recover somewhat. That's when he picked the lock, and we escaped in darkness down the beach near Llao Llao, the giant summer gambling hotel nine miles west of Bariloche.

I had to tell him about when I'd first arrived there in Rudel's Porsche. He had brought me upstairs to the grand ball, where a man who looked like Hitler had grabbed me by the ear and said to the others, "See hear, this ear is just a trifle smaller than the other, and this is why we shouldn't trust him!"

The Israeli was dying, I was sure. And he knew the wound to be mortal. He was rambling on incoherently about his family, who had all been killed in the Seven Day War in 1956. He had lost them all but could hear and see them all dancing on a distant beach somewhere where he was going. And then he went there as he died, turned to a cold stone, after pointing his gun at me and saying that I was one of them, so he should shoot me!

I had to leave him and walked through some woods, where I found a road. Then, out of nowhere, it came with its headlights glaring—a silvery Porsche. And the familiar voice said, "Get in. I'll take you home."

Too much fun (?) for one night. I now had to go back to somewhere, but I passed out cold from exhaustion.

JAMES AND JOHN

THEY WERE JAMIE ARNOLD AND JOHN STIRLING. THEY BOTH WERE SKI racers like me, they both loved their dogs as much as their women; I went with them to the Colorado Cup at Winter Park in February. They both enjoyed reefers, long cigarettes of marijuana that everyone in Aspen rolled into "joints," as that was the new trend in those days. The idea was to be like "The Beatles" in England, long-haired rock stars on the world's fresh stage.

Certainly, we all were ourselves on that glorious day. I had already won the Steamboat classic slalom, while being threatened with disqualification by the chief of the course, the US Men's National Ski Team coach, a cowboy named Bill Marolt, if I were to wear my dirty blue jeans in the second run. His uncle was Max Marolt of Aspen, who would one day die of a heart attack in Las Lenas, Argentina, taking too many nonstop runs in a row without resting and drinking enough water. So I promptly put on my ski pants for the second run and then won that race.

Luckily, here at Winter Park, it was a different set of race officials, as we were all stoned out of our minds from the pot, which was much stronger than we had smoked in quite a while. It might have been "Panama Red."

In any case, I had narrowly won the first run after John Stirling had insisted I eat a huge pancake breakfast to satisfy my id so it would not trick my ego by rebellion, hooking a ski tip on a slalom gate or some such. John Stirling was reading back-to-back books by Gurdiyev and Ouspensky called *The Third Way* and filling me in on every minutest detail while passing a joint in the car. "Smoke some more of this before the second run; it will calm your nerves!" Ha.

I remember Jamie James Arnold had fallen the first run after hooking a tip. He was more of a downhiller and didn't enjoy slalom. John was in fourth place, as he had skied the permanent course I had set in the glade, high in the Sunlight Ski Area. It was in the woods, where we thought no one else would ever ski, hopefully, as our treed slalom up there had seven-foot-high ruts from making turns in fresh powder after each snowstorm. I think we only sideslipped it once the entire winter.

Some poor soul, a middle-aged powder hound and probably a desk jockey, skied on it later that winter and hit a wall of snow, breaking his leg. The ski patrol then launched an investigation into who had designed this hidden bobsled run among so many trees, and a few chairlift witnesses had remembered seeing me and John in the vicinity. James knew better than to ski my suicide course—oh, well.

So the second run, John and I arrived at the start very relaxed, almost to the point of falling over in the snowdrift and taking a short nap. I remember not pushing hard enough out of the starting gate. But it was a very smooth run in all that freshly fallen snow. And I managed to hang onto the lead by a tenth of a second ahead of Eric Poulsen and Dan Mooney, both of California. My win propelled me into a tie for first place in the points for the High Country Trophy, the overall title for best skier in the Western USA.

I am fairly sure that onlooking coaches from reputable colleges like the Universities of Denver, Colorado, and Wyoming knew exactly our game plan. We were the dirty hippies that their parents had been very afraid their own children might become and drop out of society altogether in a ski town like Aspen.

John Stirling was anything but a dropout. He read Gurdiyev and Ouspensky on his every ride up every chair lift in existence, plus an encyclopedia of every other book ever written. He was a subdivider of real estate and builder of fine homes on Missouri Heights that resembled Yankee Clippers that had grounded in the Rocky Mountain foothills, with copper roofs and marble sink tops. James Jamie Arnold was his first mate and top carpenter, and I was their tagalong laborer of sorts, as I helped Joe Baldwin, their neighbor, who pirated abandoned mines for every last thread of steel with his Burma jeep.

Joe Baldwin was from Arkansas and was last seen a few years in a dead run for the summit of Mt. Sopris, elevation 12,999 feet, towering above 7,000-foot Carbondale. Joe had taken a bit too much acid and kept running out of sight, with everybody far behind. He was a follower of Ken Kesey, perhaps, and so died of a massive heart attack.

John, out of pity, had sold him one of his cheapest, least desirable building lots. And Joe had built a gargantuan house that looked more like an erector set sprawled up a hillside in Clear Creek. His daughter lived there in the house with him after his wife had gone raving mad at him living there and ran off, maybe back to Arkansas. Colorado can be awfully cold in midwinter, which lasts over seven and a half months. Summer is the 4th of July—until the 5th, when it snows again in the high country.

John held onto fourth place, narrowly missing a podium. He was a very strong fellow, both a wrestler and boxer at University of Utah, with his neighbor Carl Monahan, whose daughter Kater made the US Ski Team a few years later. Kater was quite an attractive blond with good taste and a sharp dresser, very important with those fussy race officials.

Now I have told you some of the history of Missouri Heights in Carbondale, which is rich and deep. John had three daughters by Ruthie, a Penn Dutch College grad from Philadelphia and a sharp dresser. James married and had a beautiful daughter by his second wife and worked himself to death, as all carpenters do eventually. He is still driving his Mazda with a Wankel jet engine spitting liquid gas out the tailpipe up in heaven. He finally sold that car, as it lost power and, with one good backfire, might have self-ignited and blown all its passengers out the front windows whichever. I sent a copy of my new book to James after he didn't reply to my phone call a year ago, only to have his wife call me in the middle of the night to tell me he had passed away just last August.

John too has left us prematurely in a car accident, not his fault, after he sailed around the world with Crazy Charlie and Olaf in the Sea of China, where their ship was cut in half by a Soviet Destroyer in thick fog. They had all lived through that. We are not too long for this world.

How sad. But at least there is a rich folk history of all these very fine and dear people. I still and always will love them dearly and have so many fond memories of them. Rest in peace, my angels. You were the saints.

Then we drove back to Aspen-Carbondale-Basalt, stopping at a tavern, which was the only business then where the giant keystone ski area and village now exist. John bought me a steak for his coaching me and my coaching him. I hadn't eaten in three weeks. Slalom skiers back then were very skinny, starving beings—like Larry Keenan, the Flash of Tabernash, who had been winning the college ski carnivals but quite often fell in the second run of any national slalom race. There were Gerry Shimer and Scott Pyles, who would have won the overall, as they not only won the giant slalom races but placed well in all the downhills. There were a lot of Californians, like Craig "Doc" Halliday and "Bif" Gotchy, his sidekick. I will look up all their addresses, but many have already passed to the angels, as did Carl Monahan recently as well.

I had a mustache back then that I had cultivated to look like a Mexican, just to psyche out the competition. *The Denver Post*, a right-wing Republican newspaper, quoted my former ski racing friend Roger Little of Montana as saying, "Cullman is an Eastern flake, a good-for-nothing vagabond whose only knack is slalom because all the other racers fall in that event!"

Thanks Roger for filling them all in with Western bias. We had been buddies once at the National Training Camp at Vail in December. We often skied that course like a Chinese Downhill, as it's sometimes called, when our skis even touched—which made us laugh at sixty miles an hour, as we were young and crazy back then.

STOWE

Duncan Cullman <dthacul@gmail.com>
Sat, Apr 20, 2019, 7:55 p.m.
to me

FOR ME, WHEN I WAS YOUNG, STOWE WAS SOME MYSTERIOUS FOREIGN place where white rich people wore mink coats and arrived in limousines. I went there to ski one weekend when my father was too busy in New York, so he sent me with Milton Hewitt, a really tough New Yorker kind of a guy. Hewitt looked like he could have been an FBI agent and probably was. But his daughter was Millie, a nice gullible girl a few years my senior. Maybe she was fifteen. And she had a crush on Marvin Moriarity, the son of the local hat maker. He was an aspiring downhill ski racer about to make the Olympic team. She looked for his ski tracks in the snow.

"Marvin has been here," said Millie. "See those straight ski tracks like figure elevens; he schusses everything!"

So we skied very fast, trying to catch up with Marvin. But he was much too fast. And Millie eventually married someone else from Stowe but not Marvin, who moved to Florida later in life with some hot, rich blond tennis star. They still play tennis there and in Stowe in summertime.

I was in tears after being chewed out by Millie's father because I was cold, having not brought enough warm clothing. He realized the mistake and comforted me, saying that I was not that bad a kid after all. But he was lying so that I would stop crying on the seven-hour car ride back to Connecticut. I slept solidly, as the car heater felt like the second coming of our Lord and savior.

So I never went back to Stowe after that until I was eighteen, with Connie Hendricks in her Volkswagen bug. She was a sweet blond young lady from Oberlin College in Ohio, and her father was an associate of my grandfather MacBride somehow, who lived in a house in the middle of the road in Hudson, New Hampshire. Eventually, the state straightened that main highway, and the house was gone. So was her father too. But Connie brought me to Stowe so we could race in the very prestigious Stowe Cup, won by Billy Kidd and Marvin Moriarity and the like.

Connie announced to me that she would be staying with her boyfriend, maybe Eric Reid, a Dartmouth ski racer, so could she drop me off at some motel? I confessed I had only one dollar, and she said I could stay with the Catholic lady in her burlap bunk room at her house, which featured no sheets on the beds and mostly late-night drunks and bums with the influenza.

I relented and let her have her way, as she picked me up seven o'clock sharp. We went up to Spruce Peak, where I won the slalom race, beating Helmut Schranz, ranked twelfth best slalom skier in the world on the FIS point list. I also beat all those important rich white college ski racers. I wore a black logger's hat that made me look like a state trooper out of *Mad* magazine.

That's all I have to say about that. Unknown to me was that Connie was my fifth biological cousin in some mysterious way. She was such a lovely young lady but already light years too mature for me.

GERRY KNAPP, AKA "THE KNAPPER"

I WAS STILL A CHILD AT BROMLEY MOUNTAIN IN VERMONT WHEN MY FATHER, struggling with his stem Christies, and I in my snowplow schuss going straight down encountered a bamboo slalom course set for the Rice family, father and two sons. They all wore those old slalom hats with earflaps and visors like baseball hats but made of leather, not cotton. The slalom poles had little flags of three colors, blue, red, and yellow, attached. It looked like fun, so I skied by a few of those flags in imitation but was soon yelled at to stay off their course. It was a wake-up call that skiing was for the rich and Anglo-Saxon, my father told me, but added that Austrians were by far the very best skiers on this planet.

At prep school, I felt some of the same prejudice when issued my first jumping skis, the bear trap bindings of which were mounted two inches behind center of my pair. No one took notice of this for three dismal weeks, during which my ski tips dropped upon takeoff, and I landed and cartwheeled on the knoll. My ski jumping career was not looking very promising, as I was immensely discouraged and soaking wet, my clothes full of snow from back-to-back crashes.

My roommate that first year at Holderness was a Pakistani who prayed every early morning to Mecca, a faraway place where Allah was God. Eventually, I would teach him to fight our English teacher, Fleck from Bowdoin College in Maine, where just white people went to school.

The winners of the Eastern Junior Championships were all Anglo-Saxon, Irish, or French Canadian American. It, skiing, was the last great white hope, with blond Penny Pitou from Gunstock, New Hampshire, winning silver medals in the Squaw Valley Olympics. White people everywhere had money and sports cars and went skiing on weekends. Nonwhite people lived in ghettos, and their children played basketball and ran track, and just a few were inducted into baseball. Mickey Mantle was my favorite, until Hank Aaron hit that ninth inning home run to beat the New York Yankees. Hank Aaron was dark as night itself. Then the So-Jo kid, Willie Mays, ran deep into the box in center field and caught a deep fly ball hit over his head that no white person had ever attempted to catch in that fashion, and the Giants won the World Series.

There were some tough and mean boxers who were also African American. But nobody dared say anything about racism in sports until Cassius Clay changed his name to Mohammed Ali. I never should have listened to him, as identifying with those poor underdogs gave me some strength but led me into an identity crisis with my Anglo-Saxon teammates on the US Ski Team, who presumed I was neither Catholic nor pure white. It was my young, undeveloped, immature brain that detested them, like the Rice Brothers, who had yelled at me to stay off their Anglo-Saxon slalom course.

I wanted to ski, and I wanted to win slalom races, because deep down inside me, there was a fighter; and losing was not in my nature.

"Hi, I'm Gerry. Get in the car!" said Gerry Knapp, who was also a ski racer. He was from Stowe, at least temporarily, as his sister had moved there and married a mob boss he said.

"Really?" I was naive. Why would a mob boss live in Stowe? I wondered, having seen them mostly on television or on newsreels at the theater.

Gerry Knapp was older than me by four years chronologically but from a very wise mix of races, Jewish Yugoslav and some Saxon back there somewhere; the Knapps were Austrian. So we had a lot in common, racing against the Anglo-Saxon rich kids, many of whom were raised with a Saxon work ethic and soon dropped out of the sport to take jobs, marry, and raise children. Not us ski bums; we were enjoying the sport too much.

Gerry said, "Take a hit of this reefer."

And I did, but it wasn't my first.

Rebel Ryan had passed me my first joint in Boulder, Colorado, two years before. Then we'd dragged a thirty-foot horizontal Christmas tree into the house through several doorways until it had become stuck, and the doors wouldn't close.

"How much money did you bring with you?" Gerry asked me somewhere near Indiana on our drive out west to go race Aspen and Steamboat in the national races called the Wild West Classic—Bear Valley, CA; Jackson Hole, WY; Steamboat CO; and so on

"Well, I have twenty-two cans of kippered snacks" (*in tin cans) "and, whoops, only seven dollars." We were indeed the poor kids en route to race the rich white kids.

"O my God," said Gerry and mused a while and then stopped for gas and coffee.

"I'm not going to kick you out of my car here in the middle of nowhere," he finally said, adding, "Do you have some friends out west where we can stay when we get to Aspen?"

"Well, my friend John Stirling has a place near Carbondale on Missouri Heights. And I have a girlfriend who is going to school in Steamboat if we get there named Wendy Coughlin."

We arrived in Steamboat, where Wendy said on the phone to wait till after dark and use the hidden ladder to climb into her second-floor dorm window. She got expelled for that eventually but said college didn't agree with her lifestyle anyway.

At the end of that long ski racing season, the Knapper showed up in North Conway and said, "Get in my car."

I did.

He then added that I owed him, and he had been instructed by his bosses to drive me to Stowe nonstop because "they" wanted me not to race in the final race of the year, the Mount Washington American Inferno. I didn't try and jump out, because I knew I had to go retrieve a Peugeot racing bicycle in Stowe that had been delivered to my client but not paid for.

"Well, if you are down and out with no money and no career and no future, you can always join the family," said the man in Stowe from behind his thick glasses at the kitchen table.

The next morning at five o'clock, I found my way out of the house and had that bicycle somehow; maybe someone dropped it off for me. It was April 23, 1969, and twenty-six degrees with a dusting of snow on the road. And I escaped, en route to Plymouth, New Hampshire, 110 miles away. I got within 25 miles when my hands froze. Somebody made a telephone call, and John French came and picked me up, wondering just what in hell I was up to.

The next morning, after a six thirty breakfast, I began pedaling toward Meredith, New Hampshire, where, frozen again, I called Wendy Bryant in North Conway, my landlord. She sent Danny Del Rossi to pick me up on the highway in Chocorua, New Hampshire, on my bicycle. It was two days before the Inferno Ski race. My frozen hands would possibly have time to heal.

LOUIS, MY FATHER

AT THE TENDER AGE OF FIVE, MY PARENTS, LOUIS AND THAIS, INFORMED me that I had been adopted and that they weren't my original parents, whereupon I began calling them by their first names.

For a woman, my black-haired Thais was a real monster. Luckily, she had a sweet disposition half of the time. But the other half of the time, when I refused to eat my burnt, overly cooked lamb chops, she spanked me and tossed me back into my crib. So I too was a little monster in her image.

My father came home every evening from New York on the train (which I had yet to discover) and appeared at the back door. She would sometimes lock it, as her lesbian friends were retreating out of the living room by way of the front door.

Then one day, an ambulance came, and they carried my mother out the front door screaming. She didn't want to go to that sanatorium in Stockbridge, Massachusetts.

My father looked at me with terror in his eyes and proclaimed, "Now you'll do what I tell you to do!"

Hardly.

So he took me with him to Washington, DC, where he applied for some government job in a very big building. I had to wait in a room somewhere until he returned. Child abuse—they didn't have a name for it back then. You did what you were told or got beat up. In Sweden, they were trying something new and experimental called child psychology. But in America, well, here we did everything with B-52s—dropped bombs on them all if they wouldn't agree with us. Yes, and if they might persist, there was the atomic bomb. *Bang!*

On a casual drive through Jefferson, New Hampshire, en route to see my grandmother Darthea in Mooselookmeguntic, Maine, my father had to inspect a hotel that had been burned down by Sugar Hill resident Joseph Kiernan of the Boston Common Garage embezzlement scandal for the insurance money. My father wasn't very thorough, because, he explained to me, he didn't want that job with the FBI they wanted to transfer him to.

He had a job with some other department of government. I was very little still and didn't quite understand. We would go to Lexington, Kentucky, to meet his boss and then to Germany, France, Switzerland, Italy, and Spain—all part of his job. I never saw him work, although he attended meetings. He had been a second lieutenant in World War II, which he had fought in Algeria in a weather station, making forecasts for the invasion of Sicily and so on. I was later to understand from my history books that that was a very big world war, which we had won. So I should be very proud of my father.

But deep down inside, I was already a communist, although not a registered communist. My father kept talking to our ski instructor, Miki Hutter from Austria, about Skorzeny's military exploits, rescuing Mussolini and so on. But on television. I saw Germans in uniforms, and they were all the bad guys, I thought, especially the Japanese. We were taught racism in school—to hate our enemies.

But in church, we were taught to love our enemies. I had gone to a Danny Kaye movie with my mother before they carted her off. Frank was an avid. Wonderful, wonderful Copenhagen. The movie showed how wonderful the Danish children were. I wanted to go there. My mother said they wouldn't like me there because my father was Jewish. It was a truly confusing world, especially for a little monster in the making.

But now my mother was gone, and in her place. there was a whole family of house servants, the Groves from London. Evidently, my father sensed that, since I was of English (mostly) extraction, this stable family would be a good influence on me. And he was right. Mr. Groves was an avid athlete, a gardener, a roofer, and a soccer player. He soon coached the Masonic little league team, starring his son Graham and me. Mrs. Groves, Caroline, baked chocolate cakes and cleaned our house.

I took Graham on a ski adventure when it snowed. We went to the country club golf course hill, where he skied over a sand trap, was unable to turn, and crashed headfirst. Yes, there was blood, and his mother wasn't too impressed, grounding him.

I was eventually shipped off to a prep school in New Hampshire at age thirteen because I was continually fighting at school. That's when my father met a divorcée named Dorothy the Witch I thought. She was after his money, but of course he didn't ever have any—until his father's will was settled. And then every bitch in hell was turned loose, and they all wore a lot of makeup and had ruby red lips and a lot of hair like my mother, but they shaved it and wore excessive perfume. Disgusting to a thirteen-year-old.

Then I turned fourteen, and it somehow all made sense. The Groves all became history for me, as they moved to Narragansett, Rhode Island, near the beach somewhere.

I went to Chile with my father, where he met some tall bald man with a German accent near Llaima Volcano. We all skied. But the lodge was very smokey, and I got the flu, while the adults climbed the volcano. The tall German looked a lot like our distant neighbor from Pound Ridge, New York, who had beautiful blond daughters and golden retrievers. His wife, bald man, invited me to come ski race in Argentina, which was very orderly and so against my father's wishes. I boarded a train for southern Chile to join up with the Chilean ski team, all young boys and girls, and their chaperone. Mrs. Leatherby was the wife of the owner of Farellones Ski Area, Chile's very first. She had been a ladies' golf champion of Chile under her maiden name, Gazitua.

Over in Argentina, I was to stay at the very friendly but not really very friendly at all Syrian Auchless or something Refugio for refugees of the war (they lost). An Israeli showed up with a gun. I had met him, evidently, in Portillo, Chile. Now I wanted to forget him. But the gun was loaded and cocked.

"OK, you can spend the night," I agreed.

My father's friend, Dr. Little in Bozeman, Montana, sent a kindly telegram which stated,

You have been kidnapped>leave at once>get on the first train to Buenos Aires. Tell them you have a family emergency you must leave>Or tell them nothing at all. Just go get out of there!

Dear, Louis, I'm having a good time here in Argentina. There is more snow than in New Hampshire, and the mountains are bigger. I may never come home at all. Well, I will when I run out of money. But it's not costing me much at all. And besides. I don't like stepmother all that much. But I see why you do—big teats!

My Grandmother Wolf was very anxious for me and hired two operatives to rescue me, all for a big sum of money of course. They were brothers of the same father and I never learned their put a hit on me much later.

I was young and naive, not exactly all my fault.

My father visited Paul Valar in Sugar Hill and accused him of hiding Nazis, even though he was Swiss, and his wife, Paula, a bronze medalist from Czechoslovakia. They had no idea my father was the US government, at least not at first. The government wanted all those German patriots down in Argentina and Chile to kill communists. Our beloved government was still at war.

BILL ASCENDING

FORTY-EIGHT HOURS HAVE PASSED. IT IS THE THIRD DAY, AND MY ROTTWEILER is consoling me over the death of my rival friend Bill McCollom, who was one year my senior at Holderness, where we really didn't like each other very much. No one expected him to die so suddenly.

I sent him my poetry book, and maybe that didn't help him at all. We were such rivals over fifty-nine years, though, for some of those, we were doing different leagues of competition. He went ski jumping, and I went professional slalom. Neither one of us made the Olympics, though our dreams were indeed that big. He managed to complete his education at Middlebury College, where I had originally wanted to go. But the school never gave me the time of day; nor did Dartmouth, as, back in those days, they were 95 percent white.

I don't need to overthink this story much. Bill's best friend at Holderness, Terry Morse of Aspen, almost died skiing into a tree at Jay Peak, Vermont, where it was twenty below zero. My father saw the accident from inside his very large fur coat that wouldn't even keep him warm. A tree branch went through Terry's jaw. And the cut the branch with a chainsaw, taking both the branch and Terry to the hospital. He lived. Bill and Terry were avid ski jumpers. I didn't excel at Nordic skiing but was expelled from Holderness for flunking English. I taught my Pakistani roommate David Nichols to fight, and he attacked my bully English teacher Fleck. I suppose I got the blame for that too.

My rottweiler looked out the window at the clouds. Bill McCollom is risen and gone to heaven, where the music of the angels and their language is of such beauty anyone hearing it would never want to leave there in the first place.

We have all been sent to this earth by our heavenly Father to learn perfection and grace. Bill learned it with a 4.0 average. He mastered the lesson here and so has risen. Most of us, so they say, will not make it where he has now gone. It is very brilliant there near the Lamb, who sits upon that throne at the footstool to God, whose radiance and truth is blinding. For He is all knowing and has every eye, seeing everything and knowing everything. Now he congratulates Bill McCollom, who has a new name like "saint." And the Lord is very pleased with our friend who once was Bill but now has risen.

Meanwhile, back on Earth, a very dismal place by comparison, eighty-eight volunteer utility outfielders need be found to take Bill's place on the mound and in the dugout as manager as well.

The water boy has been given a glove and was just told to play right field.

Of course, meanwhile back in heaven, they are playing "Ode to Joy" and Handel's *Messiah*, as well as Mozart simultaneously. All this music miraculously blends together to make a sound far too sweet for human ears. It seems God needed a new manager for heaven. So he recalled "Bill" from Earth, that very morbid place of untold human suffering.

MOMMY'S TART AND JAM FACTORY

When Mommy came to town,

She brought jams, jellies, and tarts.

Wasn't long before Daddy took notice.

Down-to-business, nose-to-the grindstone Mommy,

She wanted to make her mark in the world

And then take it to the bank and cash in,

Procure good credit and live in a very big house

Next to the post office, shipping and receiving.

She would receive dedication and devotion

While spreading her contagious love

For all creatures big and small,

While breaking for small animals on the highway, even insects.

Reptiles included, armadillos and guinea pigs, marmots and porcupines.

Birds built nests in her window, where the storm window was missing.

They hatched their young, which flew into the driveway

To watch Daddy barbecuing some kielbasa and bratwursts.

She brought her eleven-year-old cat with her, which Daddy's dogs soon respected,

Even admired when, home alone, the kitty took charge of those dogs like a pet sitter.

Mommy was down at the farmers' market downtown;

She had a heatstroke complicated by COVID-19 pandemic.

Now she is back in heaven with the angels, still busy as a bee.

Definitely not enough jams and jellies in this world short of sweet tarts.

Writing all these verses, I've grown hungry and have decided to make toast with butter.

There are thousands of jars of jam and jelly, no shortage whatsoever.

She's up there with God at shipping and receiving,

Still spreading her love to all creatures great and small.

NOW THAT MAN IS AN ALIEN ON HIS OWN PLANET

With fossil fuels industry lobbyists and resultant global warming,

Man is now an alien on his own planet.

The wet climates are wetter, flooding, and the drier climates will all be desert wastelands like Texas.

Is there any hope left anywhere from these tornado hurricanes?

Locusts, viruses, and ticks follow the dengue and yellow fever and malaria.

Earthquakes come from fracking for oil and class five and six hurricanes,

While the polar ice melts and glaciers recede. Where will this all end?

There is no planet B for the vast majority of us, only for our president,

Only for the CEOs and lobbyists, who hide in their second-home luxury condominiums.

Maybe I can find my own personal spacesuit on eBay or Amazon,

Surf the web because surfing in the ocean will soon be too dangerous.

The tsunami is coming to sweep us all away for our giant misadventure with fossil fuels.

We never respected our limitations. We never have been held accountable, so our children and future generations

Will pay dearly for our grievous existential greed.

MY CANDIDACY

My candidacy for president will be complicated

Since I am no great orator, mostly deaf and dumb.

I have been through and seen a whole lot in my long life of 72.7 years.

Perhaps I can hire a robot to make my speeches, since I cannot speak myself but can scribble notes;

I could write a script for some good-looking young actor and give him my expert advice on how to campaign:

Smile a whole lot and have a good dentist like Joe Biden and say very little.

The more you say, the more the stock market jumps up and down. So just say,

"Good evening," or, "Good morning," and, "I am your president here to serve you, so please write soon and tell me what's best!"

We all know what's worth, and that's having a blabbermouth in office.

So vote for me, because I am a nicer guy and a good guy who will make the right decisions.

The first thing to consider is the extinction of our species due to global warming, viruses, plagues, and locusts, following earthquakes and hurricanes after massive forest fires.

So if you pay taxes, let us consider where they are going and for what purpose.

GOD WILL PROVIDE A ROOF FOR YOU AND ME (I FELL OFF THE ROOF!)

I fell off the roof, but a tree saved me, as its branches slowed my fall.

Still I was very hurt and did not continue being a roofer.

Sadly, I had no other skill besides skiing and writing.

After six years of employment as a ski instructor at Telluride resort in Colorado, they fired me.

I suppose I lost focus after six or seven days without one day off,

I still have a pen or two, and no one has taken them away yet.

Guess maybe it's my God-given gift to write these verses thanking God.

Be thankful if you have any skill at all. Remember me;

I made it through high school just barely, with a few college credits.

No other skill but writing, since, after reading Dostoevsky at age fifteen,

I decided, above all else, to be a writer and continue to ski in winter, even without a job.

You are still reading this because your life is somewhat similar.

Remember me and please keep trying; do not quit.

God will find something for you to do so that you do not go hungry.

Perhaps you can cut grass or be an assistant or helper like me.

Help all who ask for your help; that is your mission in life.

Be a friend to everyone who requires you, as you can do nothing more important than this.

Then God in Heaven will be your friend, and with God, all things are possible.

Friendship is the highest ideal and more important than romance.

Why break your heart over and over while breaking others'?

The only couples who survive are best friends first and foremost.

If you are an honest person, you can keep your friends;

You cannot swindle your friends by being honest.

Why would you try to deceive God, who knows everything?

God will keep you safe and enclose you securely in his house.

He will always prepare a room for you, my good friend, and all his friends will be yours also.

I LIVE IN AMERICA

I live in America. It's just like other countries in many ways.

I go to my job every day to earn some fun tickets.

Of course, I must feed my family first, pay the rent and the bills.

I have a car too, but it's owned by the bank really.

I send out my payments to everybody, even for television,

Heat, and lights. Then off to the store to buy food.

At least we have food here, as I hear that, in many countries, most people are starving.

I am tired at the end of every work week, so I mostly rest on weekends and watch television.

If I were rich, I'd read a book. But I'm not, so I read the classified ads.

I never have enough money to pay the prices some of these people want.

So I live more off family charity, as my aunt no longer drives, and she'll give me her car.

My children go to school, where they learn history and about other countries.

Foreigners would like to invade our country and eat our food.

I don't blame them in Ethiopia or Mongolia or Venezuela.

Goats and llamas give milk, and from that, we can make cheese.

We are in a pandemic here now, but it's all over the world.

Please realize in other countries that Walmartville, the name of every town here, is not really so glorious, but our standard of living is high.

We all work to make that happen, and we are, most of us, busy as bees.

I finally managed to save up some extra money, but the car just broke down and was towed; it needs tires.

We are just like everyone everywhere, in spite of what our Hollywood movies portray.

NO PATENT ON LOVE

There is no patent on love.

It is nothing new but existed before time itself.

Who are these self-proclaimed saints who claim its patent,

Who pass the plate and ask widows for their inheritances?

God has possession of absolutely everything and everyone.

Then comes Saul, a repentant tax collector,

Who interprets everything Jesus said

And adds that, if anyone should doubt him, the former shall be cast into hell.

Minor St. Paul, how would you be so sure?

There have been many great orators, like Joel Osteen and Billy Graham and Dr. Stanley.

There is only one great Saint, and He is Our God Who does it all!

Saul was indeed born again into a new, better life, transformed by God.

Even so, he has no patent on love and has invented nothing.

God, it seems, invented himself and has the patent on love, is love!

MOUNT TREMBLANT

MANY "THANK YOUS" TO MY FATHER, WHO, WITH PHIL KEAVEY, MY godfather, decided to book the Christmas holidays in 1956 at Mount Tremblant, Quebec Province, Canada.

Flying to Canada in a DC-3, perhaps one of its final flights, as the many Boeing Stratofortess bombers were being converted to faster commercial aircraft, we landed at what, to me, looked like the North Pole where Santa Claus lives. I didn't see any living reindeer. But there were plenty of plastic ones. And everyone was speaking French. It was as though we were in a foreign country. France seemed friendlier, at least warmer. Here in Quebec, it had just snowed, and all the roads were ice packed. In those days, everyone used chains, which made quite a racket. Soon it was even colder, as we were driving north 120 miles. The very cold snow was squeaky and didn't require chains.

We arrived at midnight and so had to awaken the innkeeper late, who was less than pleasant. We were admitted into cabins with beds of many blankets. There was a problem with the plumbing, as it was so very cold. I slept like a log.

At breakfast, which was pancakes with real maple syrup, there was a local magazine with a picture of a young twelve-year-old ski star, Peter Duncan. I myself, barely nine, did take note that this Canadian twelve-year-old was afforded high status as a child prodigy. Sure enough, within three years, he would be named to the Canadian Olympic Ski Team. In Canada, skiing was a sport. I didn't realize that, in my country, a sportsman's life was as complicated as winning a presidential primary. I was young and naive and fit my feet into the brown leather boots resembling then more what we now call hiking boots. Then I was found a pair of skis without edges. But at that time, I didn't even know the difference—I wouldn't until well into my third day of skiing. Another kid in my ski class group informed me that the reason the other kids were progressing more rapidly than us was that their skis had metal edges.

My ski instructor was Freddy Reich, and his skis had edges. He was a friendly young guy, picking us up when we fell and cried in frustration. After the four days of lessons, my father took me to the three thousand-foot summit after it rained and froze solid. He placed me between his legs and proceeded to struggle on all that ice, which would have been difficult even had he not brought me with him. I am sure we would have been quite a sight to behold, but all the other skiers, noting the impossible conditions, had headed for the base lodge to drink hot chocolate, perhaps in some cases with schnapps. It was quite a workout for both of us.

Later, when I became an international ski competitor, I did meet Peter Duncan in person. And all the Canadians, Aussies and Kiwis were the friendliest sort of chaps in the entire sport. The Norwegians, of course, were the most amused to find people outside of Norway participating in their national heritage.

TWO GATES INTO THE HOLY CITY, JERUSALEM

There are at least two paths into the kingdom of heaven,

Paul has made it clear,

Whether we enter the kingdom of God by love or by obeying the commandments.

If we love one another, then we obey all the laws written for our own protection.

If we are obedient and law-abiding and observe the Sabbath, then we will discover love.

For the Jews have Moses as their Saint, whereas the Christians perceive Jesus as Messiah.

There is only one kingdom. Are there not two doors into Jerusalem, a western and an eastern?

Though you are the least of Saints and less than the Major Saint Jesus, it shall not matter in heaven, only that you are there.

Or if you are a lesser Hebrew prophet, still you shall enter into the kingdom of God and be there.

For without are whores and murderers and sorcerers and every unclean thing.

God is protected by His Seraphim, and the trees of life and knowledge in His Garden are watered by His Cherubim.

It shall not matter whether you enter by the loving each other or through love of the law; in either case, you will be there.

There is no patent on love because you cannot patent God, Who is omnipresent and invincible.

Love is universal, and the laws follow it everywhere in order to protect us.

The disciples of love looked up and beheld the Transfiguration,

Which means to me that God is always here among us and has never left.

He has not, nor will he ever abandon His People. We are His sheep, and He is, indeed, our Shepherd. So Obey the laws, which are written for our protection in the land that is our safe haven.

MY GRANDMA DARTHEA

MY GRANDMOTHER DARTHEA PICKED ME UP IN LITTLETON, NEW Hampshire, and drove me to my high school graduation ceremony but, at the school, crashed into a parked car. The policeman came and was writing her the ticket, telling me to go ahead and walk into the building. But I refused, saying, "I don't get to spend enough time with my granny, and I'd prefer to stay with her."

Of course, they locked the doors, and I missed the ceremony. To add insult to injury, the principal never did send me my diploma, although it was recorded that I had graduated and won the title Class Gum Chewer.

Darthea Heald was born in the nineteenth century—1896, to be precise—in Hingham, Massachusetts, into the wealthy Heald family. They probably had a modified New England Cape with some acreage for horses, as those were still horse-and-buggy days; and there must have been a barn somewhere. Her grandfather Heald from Fryeburg, Maine, made boots for the Union Army during the Civil War. Boot making was the source of her family's wealth. The Southern Army fought mostly barefoot and won most of the battles but lost that war of secession. In the very last year of that conflict, Abraham Lincoln decided to free the slaves. It was not any original cause of that war, but universal emancipation was a very correct and timely result.

My mother, Thais, was Darthea's daughter and grew up riding horses, as did her younger sister, Jean, and younger brother, Edwin Jr., who was a bar brawler but eventually sold Pontiac cars; my father refused to buy one.

Darthea married my grandfather, Edwin MacBride, a name that was originally McBride. But there was so much prejudice against the new waves of Irish immigrants that my grandfather's family added the *a* when immigrating to Boston from Nova Scotia, a very noble Anglican and Scot peninsula of Canada protruding into the Atlantic Ocean and covered by fog. They wear kilts up there and play bagpipes. Perhaps some of them were boot makers up there, but they were not particularly wealthy, so they emigrated.

There was another rich family in Boston, the Stetsons, who bought into the Heald factory—or maybe it was a merger. Mr. Stetson was a traveling salesman with a gift of gab and connections in high places, so he more or less took over the business, Stetson Hats and Boots, while my grandfather ran the machinery, which was like a sewing machine four stories high that somehow stitched the boots.

My grandfather worked very hard and came home quite often mean, drunk, and abusive. Of course, my grandmother was used to it and fought back like a tiger, her words like sharp arrows ripping into him. Nevertheless, they loved each other, and she invested his paychecks in commercial real estate, a field here and there that would become supermarkets and malls in the late 1950s. It took quite a while to make money in real estate, but she finally did.

My aunt Jean wore tartans too, and like her brother, Edwin Jr., also known as Ned, was a scrapper who always disagreed with my father on everything, including the weather. She married a hotdog tycoon, Bob Hoss, whom I called Uncle Bob, though he always corrected me.

"I am not your uncle, but Jean is your aunt!"

He was laid off as the VP when the business was sold to a bigger conglomerate. He never did find another job beyond house husband, so Aunt Jean wore the pants. She applied for federal loans to purchase and repair historic buildings, which she then sold to buy other new historic properties. She was no stupid woman.

Uncle Bob took all three children skiing but had no common sense. The youngest, Robert Jr., fell on the ice and slid into a shogun hole at Waterville Valley, becoming paralyzed below the waist. He eventually became an architect in Denver, Colorado, marrying and raising a family. He died at fifty years old, before I ever had the pleasure of saluting all his courage personally, as I was destroyed by my own bad divorce with children.

I have the deepest respect for this family who adopted me, although there was considerable alcohol consumption by hardworking people in those days—after Prohibition, it was the norm.

My grandfather had a heart attack and died in the middle of a spat with my granny. She remarried a German American named Otto Wagner and lived twenty more years in a tiny upstairs apartment with "Wag," watching soap operas daily. The stairs became a challenge to them both. Wag played tennis until the age of ninety-five and then died a year later, about the time my granny Darthea also passed.

She phoned me near the end. "I am dying. I'm not afraid at all. It's my time to go. I've had a good life and had wonderful children and grandchildren."

"Don't die, Granny," I pleaded.

"It's beyond my control, and God is running the whole thing up there in heaven where I will soon be." A pause. "The doctor says I am too tired and must hang up the phone. Be a good boy."

"Yes, Granny."

LIFE IN PERU

SO CONSIDER PERU, WHICH CLIMBED TO FIFTH PLACE IN CORONAVIRUS cases worldwide in this 2020 pandemic. Life is not easy there, even though Peru is food rich when compared to African and Southeast Asian countries.

For a man to feed his family and purchase a car and a house, he can go to work in the gold mines northwest of Huarez in the Cordillera Blanca. For someone without a college education, this is probably the only avenue out of poverty.

Unfortunately, the gold is extracted from veins rich in uranium and other radioactive materials as well. So although these miners drive pickups and live in decent houses supporting many children, they do not live very long and die young from a range of different cancers, leaving scores of families without fathers.

In Huaraz, there is a *colegio* (high school and junior high school) for these children of the miners, who are referred to as "los Huerfanos" (the Orphans). Many of them still have mothers, unless maybe their fathers smuggled home "yellow cake," they call it in North America, which is gold mixed with uranium in their lunch pails, contaminating their homes and wives and children. Usually lunch pails and thermoses are searched but not always.

My good friend Luis Delgado was off and on as the headmaster of this school, as well as some others. His family arrived in the Americas via the Azores to Mexico, possibly even Santa Fe for a few of them who fled with the arrival of the United States making the Louisiana

Purchase. The mines in Mexico went dry, so they were recruited to work in Arequipa, Peru, when precious metals were discovered there.

This group of families all migrated to Peru three generations ago. Then more gold was discovered in Ancash Province near Huaraz, so Luis's parents arrived in Huaraz. He was a young man of twenty years when the terrible earthquake of 1983 destroyed every village in Ancash, with one glacier avalanching off the shoulder of Cerro Huascaran, a 22,000-foot peak. The pressure and heat of the avalanche turned its snow to water mixed with mud and buried alive an entire village of Jungay, killing over fifteen thousand people but sparing seventy people visiting the hilltop graveyard north of town. The rebuilt town is on the north side of that graveyard in a location safer from future avalanches.

Life is not easy in Peru. But there is yucca, a cactus plant that is a substitute for potatoes. But if you are starving and cook the unripe plants, you can poison yourself to death, and many have.

Now with the COVID-19, SARS-CoV-2 virus, there is an epidemic spread in the central market or in the small city collective buses, which transport 90 percent of the population. For some reason, the death toll isn't as high there as in the United States. This might be attributed to a wide variety of reasons. First and foremost, the Peruvians eat more fish, as well as walk everywhere. Only the very rich and/or miners have cars and pickups. Then there is the toxic yucca. Maybe its toxins slow the virus? Then there is bottled water in plastic; only the tourists can afford that. Everyone else boils their tropical water at home to avoid dysentery. Maybe dysentery slows the virus, maybe not.

I am not a scientist, and even the scientists do not know everything about this virus.

Why Peruvians fare better than we gringos here in Walmartville can be attributed to their higher quality of life in spite of their poverty. Their food is less tampered with, and they take fewer pills than we do, although they don't need a prescription for most medicines and can buy quite a variety of medicine without even a doctor's prescription.

I would go on and on about corruption here in the USA by the AMA and the DOC and the RNC. But you already know all about Walmartville. You live here, at least for a little while longer.

LOVE, I CANNOT COPYRIGHT LOVE (COPYRIGHT DUNCAN CULLMAN 2020)

I cannot copyright love.

I cannot patent love,

Because God is love, and love belongs to God.

I belong in God's kingdom, not He in my kingdom.

God is king of this earth and universe.

While I might imagine I am the king of my backyard, it is an illusion.

Love is the kingdom of heaven sent by God into His true followers.

Because they are beginning to know God, they are beginning to know love.

When we were young, our parents loved us, while some maybe just loved money and success.

False teachers and hypocrites are exposed, and their ambitions thwarted.

Presidents who do not love their peoples are soon despised, mocked, and hated.

Love does not belong to any one religion; no religion holds a patent on love.

Our One God is love, so love His wisdom and laws written to protect you with His justice.

Printed in the United States
by Baker & Taylor Publisher Services